I0774421

Coneflower Cafe

Spring 2024

Chocofpleirn Press

Spring 2024
Fiction, Poetry, and Art
Copyright 2024

Choeofpleirn Press Editors
James P. Cooper, Art & Poetry
Ruth J. Heflin, Art & Fiction

Choeofpleirn Press is a small, private press publishing literary journals in northeastern Kansas at the foot of the Glacial Hills. Our goal is to promote the best literary and art creations we can in each magazine and book we publish.

We publish four separate journals a year: *Coneflower Café* (Spring), *Glacial Hills Review* (Summer), *Rushing Thru the Dark* (Autumn), and the *Best of Choeofpleirn Press* annual (Winter). The Spring, Summer, and Autumn journals are each dedicated to one of three major genres of storytelling: short fiction, nonfiction, and drama. The first place winners and finalists of the five creative contests held by CP—the Derick Burleson Poetry Prize, the Ben Nyberg Short Fiction Award, the Phil Heldrich NonFiction Award, the Susan Hansell Drama Prize, and the Mary Cassatt Art Award—are republished in the Winter *Best of Choeofpleirn Press* magazine. The first place award in each category comes with a cash prize.

Readers can purchase individual digital issues of each magazine as digital books directly through our website. As ebooks (pdf), individual issues cost $6 each; annual subscriptions cost $24. Please email us if you would like a two- or four-year digital subscription to just one of the annual magazines.

Readers who prefer print copies can purchase individual print-on-demand magazines from Amazon. These print copies make gorgeous coffee table books and would enhance any waiting room experience.

Writers and other literary presses can also purchase classified or photo ads to appear in specific magazines in an effort to promote their own works or websites. See our website for details and the back of this magazine for examples.

Contact Choeofpleirn Press through choeofpleirnpress@gmail.com.

ISSN 2768-9999 (Online) 2768-7988 (Print) ISBN 979-8-9885631-9-8

Cover photo: "Silhouettes at Sundown" by Karen Colstrom.

Valued Donors

We wish to thank the following donors for their generous support of our press:

Christine Andersen

Karyn Bruce

Joseph Cappello

G.W. Clift

Jeffrey M. Feingold

Louise Kantro

Madeline Wise

and several donors who wish to remain anonymous.

Editors' Note

2023 was a busy year for us, and 2024 promises more of the same.

In order to promote our publications, we traveled to three cities in Kansas to talk to writers and artists, to visit with bookstores to encourage them to sell our publications, and to meet new friends and old ones. We handed out lots of bookmarks, like the ones we have included in the back of this magazine. Feel free to copy and share them.

While Ruth was born and raised in Kansas, James immigrated here several times, finally settling to live here after we had both completed our doctorate degrees in English at Oklahoma State University. Traveling to meet with various Heflin relatives as well as to vacation in rental cabins at various reservoirs along I-70 has helped us see a great deal of Kansas, but James continues to complain that Ruth has not taken him to enough places yet, so we hope to remedy that problem this year.

In 2023, we traveled, first, in the cool air of April to Lawrence, Kansas, attending not only the Haskell Nations University powwow to talk to various artists about publishing their work in our magazines, but also visiting several of the bookstores in Lawrence to encourage them to sell our books and magazines.

Later, during the heat of summer, we ventured to Emporia, Kansas—a place we had been to before to visit our late friend Phil Heldrich, former editor of the *Flint Hills Review*, but this time we went to meet writers and artists groups to talk about our press and publication opportunities—all arranged by one of our regular contributors, Karen Colstrom, with whom we enjoyed lunch. We were pleased to see with their most recent publication that our magazines, sold in a a gift store in Emporia, seem to have impressed someone at *Flint Hills Review*, based at Emporia State University, since their most recent magazine is gorgeous, filled with colorful art. A definite step in the right direction if university-based literary magazines want to continue to compete with the likes of our small, private, nonprofit press.

Finally, in early October, we traveled to Manhattan, Kansas to visit bookstores to promote our books and magazines, and to lunch with friends in Aggieville. Unfortunately, our friends do not have cell phones, so we were never able to connect in order to catch up properly, apparently just missing them after we left the Dusty Bookshelf.

Thus far, in 2024, we had lunch with one of our poets, Amy Lerman, whose poetry chapbook, *Orbital Debris*, won the first annual Jonathan Holden Poetry Chapbook Contest in 2022. She and her husband, Mike, were in Kansas City for the annual AWP Conference. It was great to put a face with the many emails we have exchanged since her win.

Such trips and visits help us remember we are dealing with real human beings—not AI—who write wonderful works and create wonderful art, not just because they want to, but also because they must. Our world is in desperate need of more great art and more great literature, so we can continue to build connections and tear down the walls separating us.

From her research on ancient cultures, Ruth firmly believes that humanity works best when we live in a democratic and egalitarian culture, since most evidence demonstrates that our ancient ancestors actually elected their leaders long before such roles became hereditary. It's time to listen to our ancestors and to join our voices and our visions for what humanity can achieve.

Here's to a great 2024 for everyone!

Contents

Art

Fiction

Poetry

Contributors' Notes   153
Ads   159

Alpha List of Contributors

Christine Andersen 63, 81
Brian C. Billings 59
Steve Brisendine 123, 131
Kyler Campbell 27, 32
Clarissa Cervantes 58, 107
Karen Colstrom 31, 46, 62, 94, 109, 111, 120, 122, 124,
Galen Cunningham 49
Suzanna C. de Baca 143, 144
Margaret Laird Dornin 149, 151
Christopher L. Dornin 150, 152
Chloë Evans-Cross 3
George Freek 91
John Grey 95, 108
Carol Hamilton 2, 11
Susan Harrison 64
Robert Harlow 47
Nancy Haskett 75
Greta Holt 17
Marcia L. Hurlow 77
E.H. Jacobs 135
Arya F. Jenkins 30
Craig Kirchner 79
David Larsen 83
Richard Lehan 50
Amy Lerman 9
Miriam Manglani 93
Patrick Manning 37
Richard Marranca 136
Kevin McNamara 97
Brian Mosher 15, 35
Devon Neal 13, 133
Claudio Parentela 60, 82, 132
Lynn Pattison 147, 148
Deborah Ann Percy 125
Jordyn Elizabeth Pimental 36, 44, 48, 80
Susan Pollet 45
John RC Potter 89
Jane Richards 57
Sarah Selim 16,76, 90
Corinna Underwood 61
Mark Walsh 121
Jennifer Weigel 1, 12, 14, 26, 29, 34, 78, 92, 134
Buff Whitman-Bradley 110
Cheri Williams 96
Hannah Woodvine 112

Beneath the Mask

Jennifer Weigel

Night Riders

Carol Hamilton

There is something mad
about a rocking horse.
My children's had slick plastic
and thick springs that sent them
flying over dream fields, away,
away from our haunted Ohio house
even as I read D. H. Lawrence's
short story of doom beneath them.
On and on they went...soon discovered
that the distance never shortened
despite all their hard riding.
That red shingled house set in the woods,
a Sears Roebuck prefabricated home
from 1910, that house creaked
at the stairway's landing,
never quite put together right.
I loved it despite all of its sorrows.
We left that house and the horse
behind forever. We rode far enough,
fast enough, hard enough to escape
at last the voices there
that would not be stilled.

Washed Away

Chloë Evans-Cross

It was wet outside, with rain from the night before, but no longer raining, and since it hadn't rained yesterday, this brings Megan back to an old memory, one in which the weather had been similar.

It had been a hot summer day in North Carolina, 88 degrees, no rain. When she woke up and looked outside her dorm room window, the gray concrete was puddled, and a light fog was lifting off the front yard of grass. She felt relieved. Maybe whatever had happened last night had been dumped on by the heavy rain and washed away while she slept. She felt cleansed.

But that only lasted through the morning. Later that day, snippets of the night before crept into her memory without permission, playing like a horror film across the back of her eyelids. The dress she was wearing. The party. The red solo cup. Then a flash of consciousness with him on top of her, her asking him to stop. Him stopping. Replaying the moment, she shivered like a dog does after a brush encounter with danger, releasing the stress of an avoided attack. After all, she had avoided it, hadn't she? He did stop when she asked, right? Her thoughts bounced around in her mind like the metal balls in a pinball machine, violently flinging themselves from one corner to another. What was it, exactly, that had happened to her? Not only was it impossible to answer the question, but it felt impossible to ask the right questions.

So, instead, she stopped. She decided then and there, staring at the still concrete outside her window, calm and hot and gray, that she would stop thinking about it.

And it worked. Megan was, after all, no novice to shoving aside her feelings and tackling life head on. If anything, her confusion and the fear of that confusion launched her further, serving as a consistent motor humming along, propelling her forward. Any time her mind would wander to What Happened That Night, her active brain would kick in to redirect it to something more productive: a Peloton class, a study session, a leadership role in one of the many college clubs she attended.

Megan had pedaled and studied and led so fast and with such fury that she now found herself in a cushy life — she had a C-suite level position in a tech company, a supportive partner, and a 14-year-old daughter, Riley. She could afford to bring Riley to soccer practice and violin lessons and spontaneous European vacations.

Her daughter said things like "Don't you think that movie was a little mainstream?" Megan's motor kept running and her family was comfortably riding along.

Despite her gold-medal performance of convincing herself that she was fine, that what happened was not going to affect her, Megan had glimpses of clarity that illuminated just how deep a seed had been planted. When the #MeToo movement was reckoning celebrities and company executives, the public commentary could set her off. Once, years ago, while bobbing on the elliptical at her cheap gym in midtown Manhattan, Megan read the subtitles that followed a newscaster who described the most recently fallen executive. She missed most bits but caught enough phrases including "outfit" and "asking for it" to put together the implications. She hiked the elliptical and her headphones up a few notches. Another time, at a party with college acquaintances, a group of guys were lamenting the effects of a recent sexual assault case. They were wondering if these girls knew how much they were ruining this guy's reputation. Megan listened and nodded and sipped her drink. She went to the bathroom and peed and cracked her knuckles. She took shots and cranked the music and danced. Each comment was another vote for the mental election she held: to tell her truth or not. The comments always convinced her not to.

Megan had been so busy distracting herself from the pain and confusion of that night that she never even thought about the fact that something like this could happen to Riley. Now, though, that possibility was looming like a heavy rain cloud overhead, following the wind, waiting to release at any moment. Just last week, Riley's teacher had called home about an incident at school. Apparently, a girl in Riley's class had sent nude photos to one of the boys, and that boy had sent the photo to just about everyone in the class.

The teacher called all of the students' parents to fill them in. The phone call included information, but it also included implications. Implications such as: girls should not take these photos, girls who share these photos should expect that their privacy will be invaded, boys will be boys and girls should know better. And although Riley wasn't involved in the incident, Megan was feeling particularly scorned after it. How, after all these years of grinding her ass off, had nothing changed? Twenty years had gone by, yet she felt thrusted back to how she had felt after That Night in college. Riley's school protected the boys' identities for reasons they claimed as *privacy* and *innocent until proven guilty* and *mistakes made on both sides*.

Decades may have passed but the implications were the same. Megan remembers sitting in her college cafeteria, listening to a heated debate take place one table down. A group of fraternity brothers was discussing the aftermath of a sexual assault perpetrated by their brother. "She dresses like a slut and acts like a slut. Why is he getting blamed for giving her what she wanted?" and "Brody could have any girl on campus. To accuse him of raping someone is delusional. Why would he rape someone when he could have whoever he wants?" and "That chick will have no friends from here on out." Megan didn't want to be shunned. Megan wanted to move on.

But today, as Megan looks out at the street in front of her house, thinking about the morning after That Night, a new thought crosses her mind. She sees a group of neighborhood boys walking by, laughing. She feels a familiar pang in her stomach. She doesn't trust these boys. She notices one of the boys is Jared, a senior at Riley's school. Riley's friend Tiffany was one of the girls whose photos were circulated without her consent, and she had only shared that photo with one person: Jared. Tiffany had immediately felt uneasy about what she had sent Jared and asked him to delete the photos. Instead, he told her he would share the photos with his friends unless she sent him more. She refused and he shared.

Megan fumed as she watched Jared strolling the neighborhood with his friends. He wore a baseball cap and violently chewed his gum. As she stood at her window, she held her coffee cup in her hands, the steam rolling slowly from the cup, weaving through her vision. As she looked at this boy, this kid, this man—what a confusing age eighteen is—through the steam she felt a knock on her heart and a calm in her stomach. She had learned to identify this feeling as her intuition, and she had great intuition. As the steam settled, so did her decision: she would take matters into her own hands.

Once, while driving to work a few years ago, Megan heard an idea on a podcast that made her hold her breath. A Rabbi named Danya Ruttenberg was sharing a new path towards repentance and repair modeled after the 12th century philosopher Maimonides. As the Rabbi explained the proposed steps for repairing harm, Megan started to cry. Here it was: the third option. In college, she thought she had only two—she could go to the police, press charges, and become a social reject, or she could stay silent. Now, though, switching lanes through her sobs, she felt a wave of sorrow for her younger self, that no one talked about these other ways forward. As Jared and his friends turned the corner down the street and walked out of Megan's vision, she set down her coffee mug on the window sill. She strode over to her office, grabbed a blank sheet of paper and a pen, and wrote.

> *Jared,*
> *I know about the photos. I know it was you. I also know that you are headed to college on a full-ride for baseball. Congratulations. I don't think The University of Florida would want someone who shares naked photos of minors as a student on their campus. It's quite a PR nightmare for them — what you did is considered a crime, after all. Child*

pornography. That girl is underage. Besides, there are plenty of other students on their wait list, plenty of other baseball stars in this country willing to take your spot.

But I'm not reaching out to you because I want you to suffer. No, rather, I want you to transform. You see, if I go to the police and have you charged for child pornography, or if I go to UF and have your scholarship rescinded, I worry that you will wallow in pity and resentment and that you won't ever change, not really. But I want you to change. I want you to realize the harm you've caused, to really understand it, and to never do it again. To go to college and enjoy life and learn and unlearn. To grow. To transform. And so I am giving you two options.

<u>Option One (circle here)</u>: I will go to the police to have you charged with child pornography. I will then go to UF with the information and have your scholarship, and I'm sure your acceptance, rescinded.

<u>Option Two (circle here)</u>: I will provide you with steps towards repentance and repair. You will follow the steps. The details will be provided as we go, but the overall steps include: #1 Naming and owning harm, #2 Starting to change, #3 Restitution and accepting consequences, #4 Apology, and #5 Making different choices. If you follow these steps, I will stay forever silent.

Please consider these options, circle one, and leave the letter for me one week from today under your doormat.

Sincerely, Your neighbor

Megan read over her letter as she finished off her coffee. It wasn't a perfect plan, there was a lot that could go wrong. But she had spent so much time with her own silence that it now felt impossible to stay silent any longer. She licked the envelope, stuffed the letter inside, and sealed it shut.

The week dragged by. "Anything on your mind?" her husband George asked.

"Just the usual gloomy things" she replied.

"What, you mean that the sea levels are rising and we're out here living in South Florida in denial?"

"Basically."

Riley asked to go to the library twice that week. "I want to figure out why poems are the way they are."

"What do you mean?" Megan asked her daughter.

"You know what I mean," she said.

Finally, the return letter came. The second option had a big fat circle around it. It was time to get started.

Step one. Naming and owning the harm. This step included saying the harm that was caused out loud, but before Jared could do that, he needed to understand the harm he caused. So Megan compiled some homework for him. In it, she included four different articles, all of which included testimonies of girls who had their naked photos shared without their consent, and the harm that it caused them. She asked Jared to read the articles and write a reply using guiding questions including, "What harm can what I did cause? Why is it harmful to do what I did? How does what I did affect someone else?" She told him she wanted the response in a month's time, no sooner, no later. She wanted him to digest this stuff. Sit with it. Process it. Reflect on it. And then, he could confess to the harm.

When she finally got Jared's reply and confession, she was pleasantly surprised. He wrote things like "I didn't realize how much this could affect someone's self-esteem," and "I shared naked photos I had of Tiffany with my friends." Could Jared be playing the game, saying what

Megan wanted to hear? Sure. But it was better than the other options.

Next up, step two. Starting to change. This one felt like the toughest to her.

"Do you think people can change?" Megan asked her colleague Melinda. Mel was whip smart but didn't rub it in your face. She wore loose jeans and blazers and was nice to people but not people pleasing. She never wore nail polish.

"Sure. But it depends on the context. You know my husband's been in recovery for 15 years and would never do the shitty things he did when he was younger. But my brother Tom? He always was and always will be an asshole."

"Okay, but like, hypothetically, could Tom not be an asshole one day? If he were motivated to not be an asshole?"

"I mean my whole family has pleaded with him to treat us with a smidge of respect, but I don't think we are a motivation for him. I'm not sure if there's anything that motivates him other than his own self-interest."

"What about blackmail?"

"Megan. This feels specific. Are you thinking of blackmailing someone?"

"Of course not. I'm just curious."

"Well as much as I love a philosophical detour at ten o'clock in the morning, we need to finalize this pitch to the board by noon."

"Roger that."

For step two, starting to change, Megan wanted Jared to do a little soul-searching. She set up a therapy appointment for him and asked that he go once a week for two months minimum. She told him to show up with his confession of harm and to tell the therapist he wanted to understand the root cause of why he did what he did. She told him that the goal of this step was for him to begin to transform. That if he ever was in the same situation again, he would act differently. And in order for him to act differently, to change, he needed to understand why he did what he did. Megan paid Stacy the therapist for each session one week in advance. With Venmo transactions that made it seem like she was Jared's mom, no questions were asked. Times like these she's glad she works in the lucrative tech industry, despite her moral qualms with the field.

At the end of the two months, Jared's step two reply came. He was having a hard time nailing down a singular reason for why he did what he did, but he had some theories.

In middle school I was never the cool kid. I moved here from Ohio in 7th grade and everyone already knew each other. I didn't have any friends. Then, in high school, I got a growth spurt and girls started being nice to me. The other boys in my class noticed and started to be my friend. When I joined the baseball team sophomore year, I felt like the other guys actually wanted to be around me for me. Stacy says she thinks I have a fear of abandonment and that I used Tiffany's photos to get leverage in my friend group. To make them like me more. To make them feel like I am cool and can teach them something. I think she's right. I don't want to be a person who has to do shady things for friends to stick around. I want to make friends who stick around no matter what.

Alright. Megan could see some progress here. A little internal reflection, a little soul-searching. Jared ended his letter by asking if she'd consider extending therapy sessions, which she obviously would. That night at the dinner table Megan asked, "What's something bad you've done in the past, and why do you think you did it?"

George said "I cheated on a math exam in high school. I knew I couldn't pass, and I didn't want my parents to get mad."

"When I uninvited Kelly to my birthday party last year," said Riley. "She was hogging all the attention, and I didn't like being around her anymore."

"I blackmailed someone once," said Megan. "It was for the greater good."

"How did you blackmail them?" Riley seemed a little impressed.

"That's a story for another day. Let's watch an episode of reality TV. You pick the show, I just need to feel like a decent person."

"You are a decent person," said George. George always said things like that.

On to step three. Restitution and accepting consequences. Ideally, this step might include paying reparations to Tiffany to go towards her own therapy, but, given that Tiffany was not privy to Megan's scheme, that option was out. After doing some research, Megan found something called the Revenge Porn Helpline that trained people on the legal and social repercussions of "intimate image abuse" or "revenge porn," so that they could then man the helpline. Megan had Jared go through the free training. She didn't want him volunteering at the helpline itself, considering that he himself was a perpetrator of this kind of harm. Instead, she had him volunteer to run a training at his school. He had to wrangle fifteen boys to attend this training where he would explain the damage that sharing photos without consent could do. He had a teacher chaperone the training and sign a form that he'd completed it. Didn't want to give him too much leeway.

At the grocery store that week, Megan grabbed some ingredients out of her normal repertoire. "What if I made a bean casserole tonight?" she asked.

"You've literally never made a bean casserole," said Riley.

"Who says we can't do things we've never done before?"

"Okay sensei."

Step four. The apology. First, Megan asked Jared to write out a draft apology to Tiffany, then she provided some guidance on how to approach its delivery. Through their back and forth letter correspondence, they settled on a note in Tiffany's locker that told Tiffany that Jared would like to apologize to her, and that she had four options for its delivery. They could meet up in a public setting and he could apologize in person. He could leave his written apology in her locker. She could come up with another option he hadn't thought of. Or she could deny his request to apologize. Tiffany went with the note option, and the following day Jared slipped his apology in her locker. In it, he provided context for his mindset at the time, what he had unpacked in therapy, steps he was taking to transform. He expressed his genuine remorse. He asked her questions: if there was anything she needed from him, if there were steps she'd like him to take to repair the harm he caused, how she was feeling about everything now, if there were certain boundaries that she needed.

That weekend, Tiffany had a sleepover with Riley. As the girls ate popcorn and half-watched horror movies, Megan eavesdropped.

"Jared apologized to me."

"No way. What did he say? How do you feel?"

The kernels pop pop popped in the microwave.

"He said he was sorry and explained what he was doing to never do it to me or anyone again. I'm still embarrassed about everything. But now I'm glad he's more embarrassed than I am. That he hurts, too."

The kernels settled.

Four and a half months into the plan, somewhere else, winter was turning to spring. Ferns were unfurling. Here in Florida, it was still hot and humid.

Jared was at the fifth step, making different choices. Megan found herself at that step, too. She would no longer hide behind her covert letter operation. Instead, her next letter was short and to the point. It read, *Meet me at the bench by the lake this Saturday, 7:00 am.*

Megan woke up on Saturday, did her at-home yoga, made her pour over coffee, put it in a to-go mug. The sun was out. She briskly walked the five blocks to the park and took a seat on the bench facing the lake.

"Hi" came a voice, deep and timid.

Megan smiled softly and patted the spot on the bench next to her, beckoning him to join her. "Hey. Thanks for coming."

"Now what?" asked Jared. His eyes darted rapidly between hers. He was trying to read her face, trying to understand how scared he should be.

"Now it's the fifth step, which is making different choices. You have this summer at home, and then you go to college. And only you will know when you're presented with another opportunity to cause harm similar to what you did before. And only you will know if you make a different choice."

"I will. I will make a different choice. I made a mistake, and I won't ever do something like that again."

"I believe you." Megan sipped her coffee. She stared at the still water of the lake, calm and clear.

"So that's it?" asked Jared. "There's nothing else I need to do?"

"That's it. I've written up a contract. You held up your end of the deal, so I'm holding up mine. I won't ever tell about what's happened." She showed Jared the contract to review before she signed it.

"Why did you do this? Give me the option to go through what I went through, I mean."

"Because I didn't like the other options."

Jared nodded.

On her walk home, Megan took the long way. She wove back and forth between the suburban streets, looking at the different houses. She noticed the pink shutters on the gray house. How had she never noticed that house before? She picked up a white pebble from another neighbor's driveway. She put it in her pocket. When she got inside her home, alive with George's music and Riley's laughter, she rubbed the pebble in her pocket. It was real and it was hers and it mattered.

Tham Luang

Amy Lerman

For seventeen days, they've lived in my eyes,
foil-blanketed bodies and toothy smiles beneath
my lids I've kept closed more, longer, afraid
to see reporters' storm forecasts, a navy seal
denied oxygen after swimming air tanks
to the cave's thirteen lodgers. *I am an optimist,*
I tell my husband, then the drive-thru's barista
who shakes her headset, as the radio drifts,
dissolves between us, I see my nephew same-
aged, impossibility, nature's randomness.

In grad. school, during a seminar discussing
"The Reproduction of Mothering," classmates
quieted me--*You can't understand; you've not given
birth"* --their refrain echoed in my second
cousin, students' confusion decades later
darkened by my husband's sleep when I
imagine others unfruitful, how the boys'
darkness and constant rounds of "Marco Polo"
loop into parents' insomnolence, if only
to plug in a nightlight, they think, to follow
welcomed shadows bouncing, illumining
dimpled limestone.

Come early hours, bamboo floors will path
your squeaky shoes toward our bed,
my prostrate body, his bent whispering
of the last five's rescue, one by one
arising from water, their eyes sunglassed
after so many cave hours, an outside
suddenly new,
exotic, flashing
smiles, cameras,
their mothers' light.

Bullfrog Blues

Jordyn Elizabeth Plimental

Sounds of Home

Carol Hamilton

The European miniaturized kitchen
left that American expat longing
for the hum of her giant refrigerator.
I, young and living in Scotland,
was homesick for the constant wind.
I missed the whoop-and-holler
of it, the whip of branches, the feel
of it touching my back, pushing
me along, hair whipping my face.
Of course, there were other things
to write home about, begging
a CARE package, superficial wants.
What did I miss after my fetal exit?
The weightless swim of it?
Is it always that wave-steady thump
of a familiar human heart?

Velvet Rose

Jennifer Weigel

Too Slow

Devon Neal

Do the flowers feel my fingertips
as I walk by, tickling their bright blooms,
purple in the gold of the day? I know
they move, so slow we don't notice,
bending their elbows toward the sliding
sun, climbing the crags of brick
of the house, or waving their vines,
nutation, seeking support around them.
I think I'm pausing for a moment
to brush the palms of their leaves,
to feel their flowers between my fingers,
but to them, are we in fast forward?
At night, long after I stopped
to feel the butterfly wing petals
of the azalea blooming in the sun,
does it slowly clasp its own hand together,
just too slow to catch me?

A Moment of Quietude

Jennifer Weigel

Dr. O'Little

Brian Mosher

One thing I don't remember is the name of the
diminutive Irish doctor at Rhode Island Hospital,

with his red hair, freckles and charming brogue.
He told us right away there was little cause for hope.

But we chose to hope just the same, for we
had never known a more hopeful man, than our father,

and because the doctor seemed so young,
what could he tell us of hope?

But mostly because
we were not prepared to say good-bye.

Ten days of worry (for us) and suffering (for him),
all hope now lost and no choices left,

still unprepared, we said good-bye
after he was already gone.

Regret? Some days, of course.
But how were we to know on that first day,

amid the panic and the fear:
tiny Dr. O'Little was wiser than he appeared.

Peace

Sarah Selim

The Headmaster

Greta Holt

"What the hell did I say now?" Jason Stevens raked a hand through his hair. "All I asked for was corn."

He joined Hans Gerber lounging outside the store by the bikes.

Hans lifted his eyes heavenward and sighed. "How did you say it?"

I said, "Do you have any good *mabele?*"

Hans kicked his bike stand up. "Let's go. You just asked a Motswana woman if she has good breasts."

'Aw, shit." Stevens slung his grocery bags into the basket. He hauled out his Setswana dictionary from his pocket. "No. See, *mabele* means corn—and breasts. Damn. I still can't keep the tones straight."

Hans struck a tragic pose. "I just know you asked for it over and over." He started pedaling. "Come on."

"Wait." Stevens turned toward the store window. With his hands together as in prayer, he pantomimed, 'I'm sorry! 'He pointed to the dictionary. Then he slapped his forehead. He knew the women were watching and laughing softly behind their hands.

"It's good you have a wife," Hans shouted back at him. Some townsmen waved vaguely, their attention on attaching a donkey in harness to the back end of a cut-in-half Citroen. Stevens aimed a grin at the store and followed Hans.

Hans clicked his tongue like an old schoolmarm. "The Headmaster of a school, and a man your age."

"Funny, damn funny." Where would Dr. Jason Stevens be without his charm? He wondered if there would be a time he would run out of patience at being laughed at.

The two men biked up the small incline toward the school. Jason Stevens, Headmaster of Delta Secondary School, wanted to get back to work. It had been a good morning at the village *kgotla*. Under the thatched roof in the open air tribal court, he'd blocked a plan to set up a bottle store near the school, and he'd talked the council into letting him start building four new classrooms.

Delta Secondary and the surrounding town separated the lush Okavango Delta from the expanse of the Kalahari Desert. The day was cloudless and warm. Playful swirls of wind lifted the sand between a few cinder block stores. The men waved to the zebra herd behind the fence at the Ngamiland Game Study Reserve. As usual, the zebra turned away but gazed over their shoulders like coy beauty queens.

"Like women," Stevens said.

"Ya-ah," said Hans.

The Batswana women were beautiful, with high cheekbones and willowy waists, and their British-tribal accent impressed the hell out of his American heart. Stevens found himself wanting to drape an arm around them, in a friendly way.

Stevens and Hans dodged a family of goats and swerved around the new, lopsided sign outside Mma Toise's rondavel that read,' Business and Professional Women's Club of Botswana. ' A big name for only the second such club in the country, Stevens thought. Its membership was just a few teachers and nurses.

"Ann joined right away." He pedaled easily.

"Ah, your wife is..." Hans puffed through the heavier sand at the side of the road, "...your best asset."

"Yeah." Ann had started to tell him something last night about the latest meeting of the women's club, but he'd fallen asleep. A Headmaster was live-in principal, counselor, and maintenance man, stirred into a dizzying concoction including international host and tour guide. Sometimes he and Ann would escape to Safari House on the tourist side of the village; alone, they could sink into malt Scotch, and he could whine until he got tired of it, or she did.

"You know." Stevens voice was dreamy. "I'm going to take a picture of those zebra, and when Mannheim makes up another excuse to get out of evening study supervision, I'll just whip out my picture and give him a load of zebra butt. And you'll notice I said zebra with a short e and no 's', and it's football, not soccer. And petrol, not gas. And you give a guy a leeft, not a lift." He glanced with satisfaction at the gate's yellow and blue portrait of an elephant frolicking in the Thamalakane River. He'd flattered the best art student.

Hans sighed. "You're good with us, Jason." He stood on the pedals and coasted. "Our Cambridge scores could beat Gaborone's."

"Not good enough." Stevens sped the last sixty yards to the newly painted school gate with its thatched roof.

"With all due respect, you've only been here a few months." Hans, winded, pulled up beside him. "Even though I hasten to say, *meinleader*, you are doing a fine job."

Stevens jumped off his bike and walked it toward his house. "I was looking in the attendance files yesterday. You know the girls 'dropout rate is much higher than the boys'. Why's that?"

Hans laughed shortly. "Talk to Mrs. Pilane, she..."

They saw them coming across campus. Boys, fists pumping, chanting, and yelling.

"Damn," said Hans. "Honeymoon's over. Welcome to Africa."

"What do they want?"

"Look, there's Kaunga in tow, trying to stop them."

Stevens gazed at the forty-some boys shouting and marching across the soccer field toward the teachers 'quarters. "Take my bike."

He strode to his Jeep, jumped behind the wheel, and turned the key. This is what he'd been waiting for. Despite his complaining, things had been too nice, people overly responsive. 'Oh, Dr. Stevens, we're so happy you're here. The school was just in shambles before you came. ' Get real.

But this was his meat and potatoes. *Come on, baby-faced boys. Meet an American principal. Let's see what you got.*

Dr. Jason Stevens jerked the gears and turned the Jeep toward the crowd. He revved the engine, then drove straight toward them.

At the sight of the big American in the noisy Jeep, the weaker-willed boys split from the group like ants run amuck. By the time Stevens jerked to a halt in front of the boys, only about twenty were left. So much for teenaged bravado.

The Headboy, Kaunga, pushed to the front. "Dr. Stevens, sir. I am sorry. I tried to stop them, but it is as you can see."

A soccer player stepped up. "Keep quiet, Kaunga. We can speak; we have the right. We do not need the Headboy to present our case."

All six feet four inches of Stevens stood. He took his time for effect, one foot on top of the Jeep's window casing and the other on the rim between the front seats. He ignored the soccer student.

"Listen up." His voice splintered the sunshine. "In America, I've dealt with students who shouted they had rights. By that, they meant they had something worthy to say." Stevens shrugged, almost to himself. "Rarely did."

He planted his hands on his hips. "But you. You are the elite. To come to this school, you've passed tests that would send American students screaming into the bush. I expect what you have to say is worthy of hearing. But—and get this straight, gentlemen—I don't talk to mobs, and I won't start now. If what you have to say is important, you'll pick a leader from each Form.

The leaders will come with well-written notes to my house. They'll meet with me in the home of my wife and my child." He was aware of playing that card. "They will sit and present their arguments in a formal manner. I will be honest in my responses."

He dropped back onto the seat in one fluid motion, revved the Jeep's engine and turned the vehicle as if to go. "And one more thing, boys." He nailed them. "Don't ever approach me with your 'rights' if the word 'responsibilities' doesn't come out of your mouths in the same sentence. Seven o'clock tonight at my house." He left them standing on the field, eating dust from his tires. They hadn't been able to stammer, shout, or speak one complaint.

Jason Stevens laughed out loud. Kids. Everywhere the same: suckers for a little good leadership. He didn't understand weak educators; he never had. The fight was worth it and the alternatives too horrible to live with. If this was all they could throw at him, things were going to be even better than in the States. His next malt Scotch would be a victory toast. Jason down-shifted hard.

He turned off the engine. Jesus, he loved it. "Botswana! Rather spectacular, I say, old chap, whot?"

"What? How did it go?" Hans had been waiting in his adjoining yard with the gate closed.

"No sweat." Stevens grinned at Hans's face and bounded up his walk. He opened the door and swung his wife off the ground.

"Are you okay?" Ann gasped in mid-air.

"We're in! First salvos fired, and the war's already over." He danced her around little Bobby's high chair.

"But Hans said it looked bad."

"Hans plays with numbers, dear. He's not," taking a step, "in," dancing a second step, "charge!" He ended with a low dip and swung her up into a hug.

Ann kissed him. "Okay, okay." Her eyebrow rose. "So you're the best in Botswana." She took his face in her hands. "Just remember, it's their country."

"Yeah, but it's my school."

After supper, Stevens spent a few minutes with his Setswana phrasebook. Yesterday, Ann told him about a student's translation of the ark passage: "...and Noah, he transported carnivorous and herbivorous animals to the ark." These kids grew up speaking their own tribal languages, then learned Setswana, and finally tackled English. If they could live inside their dictionaries, he could, too. Stevens would not allow himself to be the one-language American.

Since coming here, Jason surprised himself with the sudden formality of his speech. Hell, he sounded like that kid in junior high who got stuffed into the ball bin.

Promptly at 7:00 PM, apparently out of respect for European time, the chosen boys knocked at the door. They had dressed to regulation in blue trousers, white shirts, and thin blue ties. There were four, one each for Forms III, IV, and V, plus the Headboy, Kaunga. Stevens was amused to see not only were the younger students not represented, but the soccer kid had not been chosen. The boys must have decided this was serious work.

"*Dumela*, Dr. Stevens, sir."

"*Dumelang*, students." He ushered them inside. "*Gaetsho ke fa. Mosadi wa me. Ke ngwanake.*" He made a sweeping gesture of his house, his wife, his child.

Each student solemnly shook hands with his wife who had been drafted as a Bible Knowledge teacher. Victor Moruti and Kaunga chucked little Bobby under his chin and ruffled his hair. Bobby favored them with his newest dance, which consisted of bouncing up and down and piercing the air with screams. Formalities over, the boys and the Headmaster sat on leopard-spot vinyl chairs in the living room. Ann served coffee and cookies. The boys opened their notes and readied their pens.

"Dr. Stevens, sir, thank you and Mma Stevens for this supper. We have not eaten the school meal out of protest today." As the school's newspaper editor, Victor Moruti held the most powerful position on campus. The others nodded solemnly. "The problem is most students would rather make their own fat cakes than endure the poor quality of the meali-meal Mr. Jake serves us."

Did they ever use a contraction? Was this about the food?

"If I may speak, please," said Bareetsi Nyunyu, the school's best debater. "The porridge does not contain margarine, but we believe Mr. Jake has received a shipment from Francistown two days ago. It is suspect he uses this butter for his own family, rather than in our meals."

"And the Prefects!" interrupted Matthew Ribane, the youngest representative. "They tell the Boardingmaster when we go the Chibuku depot because of hunger, and then something macabre will happen to us." The others stared at him in something like horror.

Jason Stevens wanted to hug Matthew Ribane. He didn't dare look at Ann as he said, "Mma Stevens, get our own notebook and write, please. All right, boys. Macabre things happen to you when you go to a Chibuku depot, and the Prefects tell on you? Explain."

"We..."

Victor Moruti cut off Matthew. "Dr. Stevens, sir, Chibuku is a kind of beer. So a Chibuku depot is a bottle store, as you know. It is two kilometers away, and to go there is against the rules, as it is off campus."

He knew that.

Ann wrote busily.

"The students who go," Victor continued, "know they are committing a sin against the school rules, but most do not ever go there for the drink." He threw Matthew a sharp look. "They only want to combine a few *thebe* and eat a good meal. This is wrong, but the anger comes at the Prefects for speaking ill of us but not attempting to fix this problem of the food."

"Yes!" Matthew broke in again. "And the Prefects, especially the Headboy, think they are the Headmaster. They tell us to eat poorly-cooked beans, when none of the students wish to eat them, and..."

Victor glared at Matthew.

Stevens leaned back. Fancy English, kids' minds. "First, where is your proof none of the students are eating beans? And second, where is your proof Mr. Jake has taken the butter?"

The boys spoke at once. The evidence consisted of asking around, and somebody saying something to someone, who gossiped to someone else, who was sure it had happened.

Then the boys were finished.

"Your evidence is not good, gentlemen." Stevens almost clucked his tongue. "And yet, I might address these things with you if..."

"But then, please sir, there is our study time," Bareetsi, the debater, interrupted, "in which the Headboy pretends he is a teacher and makes strong references to our study habits." He flourished his notes in Kaunga's direction. "Many feel the Prefects and the Headboy are corrupted by their power."

Young Matthew Ribane nodded vigorously and munched his peanut butter cookie.

The Headboy Kaunga stood. He was as tall as Headmaster Stevens.

"Sir, from the moment I decided upon a path of education, I have known I would go on to university. Perhaps this is why I have been chosen as leader." The young man turned to the boys. "I have heard you murmur names against me as I go by. Often you have said threats of dunking me in the river or covering me with pig dung."

Kaunga nodded at Ann. "Since I have learned your religion, Madame, I have known there is right and wrong, not just what each of us wants at a moment." He spoke to the boys. "Wherever there are groups living together, there must be some rules. When rules exist, they must be obeyed. That is my responsibility, which I accept. Now, do you think I'm going to stop doing right because you are threatening me? No!"

"You state your position well, Kaunga." Stevens noted the boy had crossed his arms on his chest, a stance resembling his own. "Now, I will state mine. Gentlemen, first the issue of meals. Write this down, please, Mma.

Jason Stevens, Headmaster, outlined a plan in which he himself would eat with the students for a week. Then he would invite Mr. Jake to face the boys. All parties would have their say. At this, Matthew Ribane dropped his forehead into his hand.

Stevens reminded the boys of their own democratic precepts of facing one's accusers and being innocent until proven guilty. Then he admonished them to tell all the students any of them found at the Chibuku depot would be sent home, without appeal.

"But what about the Prefects?" Matthew seemed to try not to whine.

"A debate!" Bareetsi jumped up. "We must have a school debate on this issue."

Victor and Kaunga readily agreed. "It would be the fairest course."

In the end, it was decided the debate would be held on Friday before the day-students went home. The regular debate team would be changed to afford those who held opposite opinions a chance to present the arguments dearest to their hearts. Those in favor of the present system of student government would be represented by Victor Moruti, Robert of the debate team, and Kaunga. Those presenting arguments against would be Bareetsi, Matthew Ribane, and Ntikina of the agriculture club.

The boys left, still arguing. They carried a tin of Ann's almond raisin cookies and a couple pints of milk.

"Well, that was ballsy," laughed Stevens. "Kaunga's got guts, and that Victor has a level head."

"Such an assembly of masculinity." Ann began to clean up. "You were just wonderful."

Jason was never quite sure if his wife was serious, especially about him. That raised right eyebrow of hers tended to bring on ironic comments. He looked at her; there it was, floating toward her hairline. He held his breath.

"Jason, what about the girls? Shouldn't they be represented in the debate?"

"Oh, god, yes. Listen, I'll take care of it tomorrow. I'll see Mrs. Pilane, that Motswana English teacher. She's a lousy disciplinarian, but she knows the girls. Isn't there a really good student, Delilah somebody, who's supposed to ace the Cambridge in November? Hans says she has the highest female average ever in math—maths, whatever. Why didn't you remind me to include the girls?"

"I..." Ann moved the dishrag around a plate slowly. "You know, we need to talk soon about something Mrs. Pilane said last week at the professional women's..."

"Aw, crap. Now I have to change the calendar, and we just finished it. And I've got to talk to that jerk, Mr. Jake. Probably is stealing the butter." He stretched and moved in on his wife. "Let's go to bed, Mma." Stevens ducked the damp dishrag and threw it back. They tried not to wake up the baby as they tussled among the rooms of the little house.

The next morning, Headmaster Stevens mediated an argument between Swedish and Zambian teachers about which one was taking the other's South African #2 pencils, until the Swede remembered he'd lent them to a pretty Namibian teacher in hopes of a little company on a trip down to Ghanzi. Stevens organized a clean-up detail for the big toilet houses, or 'absolution blocks.' When he tried to make a call to the Ministry of Education in Gaborone, the phones were down for the third time this week.

On the way to see Mrs. Pilane, he was waylaid by a Form IV government teacher complaining about a student who had skipped class to go fishing in the river behind the school farm. Stevens wrote a punishment detail that would have the student chopping out tree stumps from 1:00 to 3:00 on Saturday afternoon.

Crossing the soccer field to his house on the riverbank, Stevens caught shouts of greeting. He kept turning, starting to wave, but finding no one. Conversations in the village—acoustic aberrations—floated across the river and echoed on the school grounds. After four months here, he was still fooled.

He stopped briefly to look at the turnip and kale shoots which, when the rains came, would be added to the school's menu. The predictions were good, and the river flowed. The school was rapidly becoming a showcase for sustainable farming. They'd make a name for themselves with the agriculture, and then hit 'em with their Cambridge scores. Stevens smiled.

The warmth of the day was turning rapidly to heat, and the odor of shredded beef on village cooking fires settled over the campus like an oily mist. A line of sweat ran down Jason's temple. It was going to get hot. He wished he had remembered one of his baseball caps.

Mrs. Pilane's blockhouse was situated under the acacia trees. Stevens admired the new white and blue paint on its door. Soon, he'd have students paint murals on the front of each classroom.

Bowing to the afternoon's rising temperature, Mrs. Pilane had positioned her class outside on the half-moon seats in the shade. She was trying to explain prepositions, as his new, Americanized curriculum demanded, and no one was listening. He watched her: delicate hands, graceful hips. As the students became aware of him leaning against a tree behind them, even the boys straightened their backs and pretended to write busily in their notebooks. Dr. Stevens's reputation preceded him.

Mrs. Pilane's voice was weak and her delivery muddled. She turned her back on the class to write each preposition on the board. Stevens found himself biting his knuckles as she droned on. Sweat started under his arms.

"Mrs. Pilane, may I?" It was said before he could stop himself.

Startled, she wiped a streak of yellow chalk first on her forehead, then down the front of her dress. "Oh, of course, Headmaster Stevens."

He strode to the front. She looked so anxious his arm reached out to her, but he caught himself and ran his hand through his hair instead. "Students, Mrs. Pilane is giving you an important list. Write it." They wrote, and he moved among them correcting and encouraging. He was back in front of the class in two steps.

"Now, with Mrs. Pilane's permission, I am going to show you how to Remember This List and Like It!" The students giggled. In an exaggerated rhythm, he chanted a rhyme, gestured to them, and they began to repeat the rhyme, substituting new prepositions. They laughed and clapped as each successive word made a different word picture.

"Now I have a challenge for you. Each of you will make a picture that corresponds to one of the prepositional phrases. Yes, you may make pictures in your notebooks."

He took the hand of a serious-looking student and led her to the front. "What is your name? Miriam? Miriam will assign a phrase to each of you. Draw carefully, students, raise your hands, and work well while I talk with Mrs. Pilane about another matter." He watched a moment to be sure the girl he had picked was exercising her authority with relish. Then he turned to Mrs. Pilane.

She had retreated to the side of the blackboard. He took her arm and guided her a few steps away into the off-concrete sand. "Thank you, Mrs. Pilane. Maybe I miss teaching a bit?" He cocked his head and grinned down at her. "You were doing a fine job."

"Headmaster, it is a pleasure to have you demonstrate for us." Mrs. Pilane's back was straight and her gaze fell somewhere between his cheek and chin.

"Well, that's not the reason I've come. I need to talk to some of the good students about a debate Friday, and I'd like you to see that some of the older girls take part. Ann says Delilah—uh, that math student?"

"Delilah Masedi, sir."

"She said the girl is an excellent student. Perhaps you could recommend a few more?"

"Oh, but Dr. Stevens, Delilah is presently in your office. She is withdrawing today."

"What?"

Mrs. Pilane moved a few more steps from the class and lowered her voice. "She has responsibilities."

"What responsibilities? This is a very good student. I'm sure we can help. Is it the school fees?"

"No, Dr. Stevens. Many of the girls who are day students take care of the young ones at home by themselves. Parents are often at the cattle station or the crop lands. The older girls take care of everything: cooking, cleaning, washing clothes. It is much work." Mrs. Pilane smoothed her skirt. "And, for some, if they are, called out…"

"Stay with it!" Stevens had turned to keep the students on task. "Mrs. Pilane, perhaps you and my wife could conference about some ways to keep the students involved. What were you saying about Delilah?"

Mrs. Pilane narrowed her eyes and stared past his left shoulder a moment, then seemed to make a decision. She began to walk past him toward her class.

"Mrs. Pilane." His voice stopped her.

Mrs. Pilane turned. "She is satisfied," she said softly, and walked to the front of her class.

"Satisfied?" Stevens was stunned. "Satisfied?" A warning nipped at him. "We cannot have good students deciding they've had enough." He snagged his sock on a thorny bush as he followed, irritated that he was abruptly in front of the class. "Mrs. Pilane, I know you, as an educated woman, support the continuing education of our girls."

The students were staring at him. Suddenly, holding back for just a split second, or at least lowering his voice, seemed awfully important, but he plowed ahead. He gestured at the girls, most of whom filled the first two rows.

"Young ladies, you must not be satisfied with less than a full education. Many of you will eventually earn a first or second pass on the Cambridge, and you will find yourselves at university, taking your place among the brightest of Botswana. I'm sure Mrs. Pilane agrees you must not be satisfied until you achieve your dreams."

The students sat. Some looked at their knees, a few glanced at each other, while others sat bolt upright and seemed to gaze behind Stevens at the orange trees on the edge of the school farm. One or two of them stared outright at him, as did Mrs. Pilane. A few students hiccuped behind their hands.

Stevens felt the sun hammer his moist neck. A thin odor from the absolution blocks seeped into the enclosure. "Well, uh, let's see the pictures you have made."

"We are still working, Headmaster," said the leader, Miriam.

He tossed the chalk he'd been clutching into the chalkwell. "Good. So. Mrs. Pilane, thank you for allowing me to visit your fine class. Work well, students, and listen to Mma Pilane."

Retreating down the gravel path he thought he heard giggling, but it was quickly stifled.

The dismissal bell rang. Sweat pricked Stevens's scalp. A large globule fell down his neck as he strode into the soccer field's clearing—*football* field, his mind corrected. He was annoyed. Mrs. Pilane's response had been terse, and he had lost the class. He hated not knowing why, but his years of experience were letting him guess. He glanced up to see two tiny dirt tornados destroy each other in a fleeting dance over the river.

"Have you noticed how we all huddle under the trees like cattle when it becomes hot?"

"Afternoon, Hans."

They stopped under a mopani tree by the field where the Delta Gold Tigers were practicing for next month's game with Francistown. Seth Harleman, the banned South African

center mid, was running drills. Matthew Ribane and Duke waved. Across the field under a large shade tree, they saw Kaunga, Bareetsi, and Victor Moruti with notebooks, probably conferring about tomorrow's debate.

"Delilah Masedi is in your office."

"Hans, what do I do about this?"

Hans draped his arms over a branch. "She has to go. The Board of Trustees will insist."

"Why?"

"She's pregnant."

" Ah, shit." Stevens sighed. "Who's responsible?"

"That, Herr Headmaster, will not be an issue."

"The hell it won't. If one of our girls is dismissed, the boy who did it is out."

Students began filling the area around the field. They called to friends and strolled past in small groups. It irritated Stevens that he did not know most of their names.

"Jason, listen. You're a good Headmaster, we need you. And none of us can say that easily."

"Well, that's nice, but..."

"Just listen to me. I've been here six years." Hans pulled his tie loose. "The Batswana are smart. They took what they wanted from the British and kept their own laws. But you must understand something; it's essential, my friend."

They watched a group of JC girls walk toward the cafeteria. The skirts of their school uniforms floated around their thighs in the afternoon heat. Stevens felt dizzy at the thought of a long, cool bath.

Hans continued, "There will be no search for the male who made Delilah Masedi pregnant. Most of the time, if a girl is 'called out' by a boy, she goes. It's mixed up with pride, fertility, duty maybe."

"Look, I don't need a lecture on..."

"It's accepted, yet it's not. Sometimes the men stay around; sometimes they don't. I've heard some Batswana blame the British, an easy target, and others actually blame the decline of polygamy for it! Hell, I don't know."

"Wait, wait."

"There's more." Hans stared at the players practicing headers. "Hints about girls being, well, hurt if they refuse."

Seth Harleman shouted furiously at a forward as the boys sped by.

"Not here. Not on my campus."

"I don't know; it probably just happens in the village. You hear things. But, in all my years here, only three rape cases have ever been tried. One had a conviction, and the man was fined twelve *pula* or three days in jail. Mrs. Pilane told me she brought up the problem to that new professional women's group last week. You know, that sign we passed yesterday."

Stevens felt perspiration spread over his chest. "Doesn't the church care about finding the father?"

"Come on, the mission board made you sit through training, too. What's more important to people: their religion or their habits?" Hans poked at the dirt with a sandled toe. "Look at these boys. Maybe one of them called out Delilah Masedi. Maybe it was an older man from town. And maybe..." Hans kicked down at the dirt so high it flew. "You hear, with teachers moving around so much. I mean, you hear about teachers."

Jason Stevens groaned.

"But she went." Hans said. "Delilah was called out, and she went. Now, it's she who leaves. That's the way it is."

"But we've got to do something about it!"

"You've already forgotten the women's group?" He dropped a heavy hand on Stevens's shoulder. "Okay, Headmaster, take on every issue yourself; take it all on, burn out, and transfer to the Ministry of Education in 'Gabs 'next year, like the others do. You'll feel righteous."

"Dammit, Hans." He shook him off. "I can't just let it go. The girl's knocked up. She had a future." Across the field, Kaunga the Headboy stood and made a sweeping gesture as Victor wrote in his notebook. "Kaunga will help me. I'll ask him to find out who did it."

Hans turned to go. "You've never heard of perks?"

Stevens sat down under the tree. He watched a dirt devil attack the little grey and white rondavel chapel building, scattering the short-tailed cats nesting in its thatched roof. The heat shimmered now, foreshadowing savage summer winds from Namibia. Ancient storms had spit the delta's thin soil onto the Kalahari Desert.

He remembered how the dust had kicked up outside the half-roofed pink church in the village the day they'd arrived. One minute he'd been greeting the minister and his wife, both refugees from Angola. They were telling him about the times they had been put in front of firing squads as they tried to get out. The next minute, he couldn't see them for the sand whipping about. He'd shielded his eyes and tried to make out the church and the people through the coarse, copper fog. But for that moment, all of them were gone.

What was it about going so far from home that made a person feel like an idiot, or more exactly, a babe in arms? Events seemed veiled in shadows, and he couldn't make out the corners. His mind squinted, and the obvious escaped him.

What had Mrs. Pilane said? 'She is satisfied.' Stevens swiped at his neck with the tail of his shirt and took out his dictionary. He looked for definitions of 'pregnant.' Yeah, he got it; he got it.

'Pregnant , adj. Become pregnant'- *ithwala*. 'She is pregnant '–*o ithwele*.

'Become pregnant, of cattle '–*nemeruhala*.

Stevens almost threw the book.

Then he saw, 'Pregnant of an illegitimate child '–*ithwala mpa ea dikgora*.

He looked up each word. *Ithwala*—'conceive.' *Mpa* ˣa belly.'

Ea—This one's definition was so long he had to guess... . 'pronoun 3rd person of nouns with no prefix for singular, but whose plural prefix is *di*; It-they.' Jesus Christ.

Dikgora—...'this word is also used to denote illegitimacy, of a child, and illicit intercourse on the part of an adult.'

The definitions for *dikgora* went on, giving the Setswana phrases for 'an illegitimate child, a woman who has illegitimate children, a loose-living woman: a prostitute.' His temples started to throb.

Where was it? He rushed through each definition again. It had to be there... *ithwala* - 'pregnant; '*mpa* - 'belly; '*ea*' whose **plural** prefix is <u>di</u>.'

Shit. *Dikgora—Kgora*! Stevens ripped pages getting to it. *Kgora*--'to be filled; to be fed; to-be-satisfied.'

Jason Stevens, Headmaster, rested his head against the mopani tree. His reputation would precede him, all right. He smiled bleakly. Through half-closed eyes, he watched Kaunga and Victor run toward him, waving their notebooks.

Delilah Masedi was waiting.

Thistle

Jennifer Weigel

To the Lifted Pickup Truck Who Passed Me Doing 65 mph in a School Zone Outside of Greenwood, South Carolina

Kyler Campbell

If the exhaust from your truck were any louder
it would shake the earth out of her orbit,
careening us all into the warm embrace of the sun.
For a few months, we would enjoy summer all year long.
And as all of creation rushes toward its final end,
soon to be cremated in the core of our very own star,
I imagine you'd roll down your window
flip down your mirrored shades,
and smile as you declare,
"Sun's out, guns out, y'all."

Or maybe your mud-slinging machine
would spin us all into the darkness of eternal space,
past the fences of the Milky Way galaxy where
rules of physics break down into mere suggestions.
While children float out of their mothers' arms and
everything green dies in the black vacuum of space,
The force of your three-and-a-half-inch exhaust
would propel us through the cosmos,
with you standing at the helm of the earth,
our mud-bogged captain,
leading humanity to eternal glory.

And eventually, maybe, our lonely sapphire of life
would come to rest at the end of the universe,
settled at the Throne of God.
The Lord would ask you,
"My son, what have you done with the gifts that were given?"
And like a self-assured toddler, you'd say,
"Behold!" and point to the legacy of your mortal existence:
A mid-nineties Ford pickup
lifted to the heavens like the Tower of Babel,
rumbling the foundations of the earth,
a testament to your will and red-neck ingenuity.

You think, just maybe, the High King of Heaven
will offer a high five
or crack a cold one
in honor of your triumphs.
Maybe, you think, he will fill every corner of his throne room
with shouts of "Hell yeah, brother!"

But I am sure that God would stare at you much like I did
as you passed me doing sixty five in a school zone,
mesmerized and confused,
with a touch of bewilderment.
And the Lord of Hosts will scoop up your legacy and your ego
and gently place his lips to your forehead,
a patient and loving father
Then gently, the voice of God will whisper in your ear,
along with every tongue in human history.
And all together, they'll declare,
"What an asshole."

Of the Flesh

Jennifer Weigel

Youthful Extravaganza

Arya F. Jenkins

I drank shots in the rain and beer in the sun
And got wicked hangovers I didn't deserve because
Christ I was young

So young I wore coveralls without a bra
No underwear and clogs in and out of bars

A disco princess
I didn't stop trying to feel everything

New Year's after bars closed
We drove to Mel's in the West Village
Waking up in time for dinner at the Lamplight

Mel's bathroom stall had a map with stars
On every port he'd visited as a sailor

I danced everywhere
S & M bars and sidewalks
Even the White Horse Tavern
Inspired by the sodden bohemia of roaches

An artist at making a fool of myself
I only grew quiet when jazz played low
On Mel's record player while the
Adults I was with sipped Courvoisier
Rapping about times long ago.

Hide and Seek

Karen Colstrom

To That One Student Who Asked,
"Can It Really Be Rape If You're Married?"

Kyler Campbell

I know you didn't mean it
the way that everyone thinks you did.
Your brain lit up in response to a question I asked,
and you answered with all
the earnestness of a true scholar who,
in spite of his own limitations,
is thirsty for knowledge and enlightenment.
And, my God, were the others were happy to enlighten you.

"Can it really be rape if you're married?"

The class's collective head whipped around,
fast enough to send the winds of first, second, and
maybe even a new third wave feminism
howling into your nostrils,
filling you with violent knowledge.
In a way, you brought this on yourself,
but I can't blame you for asking,
putting your ignorance out
into the open for others to
examine,
pick apart,
and judge.

"Are you asking to get hit?"

"Do you even know what rape is?"

"What would your mother think of that question?"

Their questions fired off
quicker than you could retract your original question.
If I were a good instructor,
I would've whistled
to end the train
of belligerent
and justified feminine rage.
But there was a lesson to learn here.

One by one the women took turns
filling you with knowledge that
you didn't ask for,
fierce and unrelenting,
plunging their words into you
until your face slumped and slacked
with the weight of it all.

And there I stood, as still as possible,
Slightly afraid, but somehow still amused.
Their explanations
definitions
experiences
blurred one into another.
until, overwhelmed by their force and persistence,
you achieved enlightenment
without even knowing
how desperately you needed it.

The Bee Has Spoken

Jennifer Weigel

Raymond Carver's Toaster

Brian Mosher

I wish I could write a poem about
a toaster, like Ray Carver would.
A toaster sitting idle on the kitchen counter
full of crumbs from old pieces of toast.
On the same counter a note,
"goodbye darling", in that
handwriting that he couldn't
help but recognize. And next
to the note a wine glass, lipstick
stain at the rim, a quarter sized
circle of wine still sitting in the
bottom. And next to the wine
glass, her key to the apartment.
She wouldn't be using that anymore.
She wouldn't be opening that door
again. Wouldn't be wrinkling his
sheets again; or smoking his
cigarettes. She'd have to buy her
Own from now on.
I wish I could write a poem like that.

Candy Clouds

Jordyn-Elizabeth Pimental

Even the Geese Don't Fly in Perfect Vees Anymore

Patrick Manning

Early on Thanksgiving morning, Ed loaded his grandson Will into his Ford Ranger and drove south on route 219 toward the Allegheny National Forest.

Will twisted in his seat and watched the white smoke puff from the oil refinery. Even through the closed windows, he could smell the stink of oil. The day before, when Will's family had driven six hours from Philadelphia to Bradford, his father pointed out the welcome sign painted on the oil drums. Smirking, his father revised the message: "Cool town, warm hearts…but it still stinks like farts." Will's mother laughed but said, "Stop it," and his father turned to Will in the backseat and said, "Don't repeat that, Will!"

Now, alone in the car with his grandfather, Will heeded the advice.

Past the refinery, the expressway ended and gave way to a winding, two lane road. Will tried to count the trees that flitted past his window. The numbers quickly jumbled together, and Will squeezed his eyes shut against the growing tally marks in his mind. Ed mistook the boy's tightly drawn face for a smile. He felt proud of himself for taking Will out into the forest this morning. The idea had come to him standing at the kitchen sink, bracing himself for his daughter Joan and her husband Damien to arrive, half-listening to Belle, his wife, ramble off the list of dishes she would make for the holiday. He thought maybe he could show his city-raised grandson a bit about the natural world. About the order of things.

With conviction, he told Belle, "Tomorrow, I'm going to take Willy on a hike."

Belle patted him on the shoulder and smiled. "Willy would love that," she said, and she promised to keep everyone else busy with peeling potatoes. She had seemed proud of him, too.

Along the side of the road, Ed spotted a grove of black cherry trees. He slowed and pointed it out to the boy. Will opened his eyes again to look.

"We had a moth outbreak up here, and all those trees are going to need harvested." He lingered on the word *harvested*, and it filled the space between him and his grandson. Will turned the word over in his mind. He imagined rows of men in overalls marching out of the forest with wheelbarrows full of black cherries. A stream of deep red syrup followed them to the place where they flipped the wheelbarrows into a waiting truck. Will sniffed, convinced he could smell the sweet-sour of cherry pulp.

Ed said, "Same thing happened with the ash trees a few years ago. They came in and harvested just about all of them." Will tried to reconcile the ash tree harvest with the image of the cherry pickers. Now, the men in his imagination emerged from dusty clouds with wheelbarrows filled with ash, like coal miners marching out of their caves.

Will asked, "Do they burn all the trees?"

Ed turned the radio down to figure out what the boy was asking. Burn them? Had he heard right? He looked at Will, who sat looking out of the window with his hands white-knuckling the shoulder strap of the seatbelt. He was a strange boy, Ed thought. Kind, considerate, but strange. They were calling it autism now, but Ed didn't believe it. The boy needed structure. Discipline. He needed someone to teach him how to be a man. The city was too claustrophobic, and the boy's father too indulgent. And Joan, it seemed, had abandoned her own upbringing and embraced Damien's urban extravagance. Once, when the boy was only two, Joan had taken him to the Philadelphia Museum of Art. Ed thought it was silly. *At that age*, he had said over the phone, *you can just take him to the grocery store. It'd be the same thing*. He laughed, and his daughter – suddenly – needed to finish the dishes and get off the phone.

Ed tried to imagine how Joan might answer Will now, wondering about burning all the trees. She usually mediated the conversations, like a translator fumbling between two languages that she barely knew.

Finally, Ed simply said, "No, they just cut them down. Harvesting trees just means you cut them down and turn them into lumber. To build with. Things like houses." Ed glanced at Will, then back to the road. Will looked satisfied with the explanation.

Although Ed was proud of himself for planning this outing, he also had to admit that he felt nervous to be alone with Will. The boy marched his two fingers like miniature legs along the base of the window and stared into the forest. Exhaling, Ed said, "You probably don't get to see trees like this in Philly."

Will offered a small shrug and looked down at the floor of the car. He was thinking of Fairmount Park and its dense forest that sprouted along the Schuylkill Expressway. He pictured himself in the tree house that cantilevered over the treetops, and he could smell the rot of autumn. From that tree house, the roar of the traffic hummed like a bird song. Will didn't know how to explain the smell and the sound to his grandfather, so he looked out the window and said, "My dad takes me to see trees sometimes."

Ed looked at Will when he spoke, but the boy's eyes were scanning the trees outside, like he was speaking to no one in particular. *For Christ's sake*, Ed thought, *Damien couldn't even teach his son to look a person in the eyes.*

He gripped the wheel and accelerated. His son-in-law Damien -- the stay-at-home dad, the med school drop-out, the social media guru, the man with painted fingernails and tattoos -- filled the road in front of him and took up all the oxygen in the truck. Ed cracked the window, and the breeze whistled in the cab. Against the chill, he gripped the steering wheel tighter and sped too fast through the intersection at Tack's Inn, the yellow blinking light only a suggestion. Ed had never felt comfortable around Damien, and the hike was as much about getting away from his son-in-law for a few hours as it was about being with Will. There wasn't one thing that had happened, no eruption of rage; just slowly, over the fifteen years Joan and Damien had been together, Ed's distaste for him grew and grew.

"When you say something, you got to look a man in the eyes, Willy." Ed scolded.

Will had heard this before—mostly from teachers. He tried to obey. He looked at his grandfather's eyes. They were staring straight ahead at the road and looked hard and veiny. "Sorry," he said instinctively. Will held his attention on his grandfather's eye and twisted his hands over each other again and again. He was not aware of his own rocking gently back and forth.

Finally, his grandfather looked over briefly to catch his gaze.

Is this what he wanted? Will stared at the top of his grandfather's nose just between the eyes like his therapist had taught him. Will told himself he needed a redo, so he shouted, "Sometimes I see trees with my dad."

Ed grimaced at the outburst. "Sit back, Willy," he said.

As the boy tried to settle into his seat, Ed swallowed his annoyance. Maybe this hadn't been such a good idea after all. There had always been a chasm between him and his grandson, matched only by the growing gulf between him and Joan. He wanted to blame Damien for it all. He had been a boyfriend they all thought Joan would grow out of; but there was the moving in together, the multiple relocations for med school and residencies, the wedding, then the baby. Damien had stuck around far past his welcome.

Ed realized, though, that it was too convenient to blame Damien for all of it. For starters, Ed hated long turnpike rides, nights spent under the glare of streetlights, and the loud neighbors at his daughter's South Philly home. Sometimes, too, he worried that his daughter had distanced herself because of his growing interest in politics. Joan was a pediatric cardiologist, and Ed felt that he had some share in her intellect and success. Because of this, he liked to pull her into political debates to prove his own intellectual acuity; she was kind and indulged him. He talked about the news of the day, but he could never quite articulate what all of it meant to him. It wasn't illegal immigration, or the liberal media, or vaccine mandates, or woke culture. Not really, anyway. But he could never quite put words to what he felt deep in his belly; it was always frustratingly just out of reach. And as he stumbled to explain himself, his daughter would grow angry or, worse, bored.

When she'd finally had enough, Joan would exhale and say, "Well, I better get dinner started."

Ed would say OK, and a few hours later send a text message of something off-topic, like a picture of the sunset, just to be sure Joan wasn't offended. She would always reply.

Ed accelerated a bit more. The speed calmed him.

"Grandpa Ed, it's kind of cold." Will hugged himself. Then, as an afterthought, he looked at his grandfather's eyes.

Ed rolled the window back up and slowed the truck. He said, "We're almost there, Willy."

Route 219 turned down a hill and, at the bottom, just before it crossed Elk Bear Run Creek, Ed turned off onto a small patch of gravel set back from the road. "I used to go hunting back in these woods," Ed sat for a moment and looked into the forest. "Long time ago it was an oil field, then the trees started coming back, and deer like young trees, so it was a good spot," he smiled, thinking back to when the forest was young. "Guess all the trees have grown up since then." He added, "Just like you," but Ed felt strange immediately after saying it; it was too cutesy, almost like it came from someone else.

Will didn't seem to notice. He unbuckled his seatbelt, pressed his nose against the window, and imagined the creatures lurking in the forest. He dispensed with the most likely candidates: deer, rabbits, maybe a bear. In the shadows lurked a centaur, the overlord of a world of elves. A dragon hid under the roots of the tree. The bare branches hid the fiery feathers of a phoenix as it surveyed its dominion. Will bounced in his seat; the boy's enthusiasm quieted Ed's doubts about the wisdom of this hike.

Ed got out of the truck and made his way around to open Will's door. "Need help down?" Ed asked.

Without answering, Will jumped to the ground and landed on all fours. Tiny pebbles stung his hands through his thin drugstore gloves, but he didn't say anything to his grandfather. Instead, he rocked from left to right and rubbed his palms on his pants. "I'm fine," he said and turned to the forest.

The trees were skeletons in the late November chill. Here and there an evergreen colored the forest with green, but mostly it was gray and jagged. The sky, though, was uncharacteristically clear and a brilliant blue. The morning light cast zig-zagged patterns across the truck. Will and Ed could see the trailhead, but it was marked with yellow hazard tape, tied around the trunks of trees, blocking the entrance. The tape looked stretched and weathered, but it hadn't yet been torn.

Ed reached down to help Will zip up his coat, but Will pulled back and bumped against the truck door. "I'm OK," he said. He pointed to the blocked off trailhead and asked, "Is it open?"

Ed shifted back on his heels and sauntered to the trailhead. There was a laminated sign nailed to the tree: **TRAIL CLOSED.** Over the summer, a strong storm had blown through, felling trees across the trail. Ed remembered the late-summer storm; there had been flooding in Bradford and reports of a tornado touchdown to the south. Traveling on the trail was unsafe, the sign said, on account of the trees, and some unstable ground along the ledge of a sheer cliff. But he didn't drive out here for nothing, Ed decided. And, besides, this was his old hunting area, a trail he had taken his own kids on for years, a place he knew well.

"Good thing for us," Ed said, trying to sound authoritative, "the forest doesn't close." He pulled up the caution tape and motioned for Will, who ducked under it and watched as his grandfather threaded his way through, careful to ensure his footing.

Ed breathed deep into his belly. The trail was narrow, but with the trees bare the path looked easy to navigate. He wondered why they had gone to the trouble of closing it at all; everything looked in good order to him. Ed zipped his heavy Carhartt jacket up to his chin. Though he seldom drove out this way, he felt a sense of control and calm in the forest. With intention, Ed reached out and pressed into the bark of a sugar maple tree. It had been almost a full year since Bradford Forest Company had laid him off. The company blamed it on the pandemic slump, but Ed knew it was a result of corporate reorganization after it was bought by a German firm. However, he had worked there for many years, so it was instinctive to imagine the tree as lumber. He looked up to the branches and read the ridges of the bark like Braille. *Not worth cutting it down*, he thought. *Couldn't get more than a few good planks out of it*. Will, a few yards ahead, had found a large stick and whacked it against the trunk of another sugar maple. Ed pushed himself off of the tree and followed his grandson.

Will darted along the trail and weaved a fantasy as dense as the forest. An Elvish spy had been sent by the commander of the Dwarf-Elf Alliance Army. *You need to get word to our troops in the west of the incoming attack from the Troll King*. Will leapt forward and whacked the tree once, twice, three times. The rhythm was predictable – a whack, a silent beat as the stick twirled above his head, then another whack as the stick landed against the tree. The vibration through his palm and up his arm was like a magic spell. The spy catapulted forward. In the tree limbs, however, a gryphon crouched with its wings tightly clasped. The elf saw it too late: he tried to cast a freeze spell, but the gryphon had taken off, made two circles in the air, and nose-dived toward the elf. Its talons sunk into the elf's shoulders and lifted him off the ground. *Where are you taking me!?* But the gryphon didn't reply. The elf unsheathed his sword and began to attack the gryphon in midair, landing blow after blow against the gryphon's leg.

"That's an oak." Ed called.

Will slowed his swings and reminded himself, *look at his eyes*. He found the spot where his grandfather's eyebrows met, but he could maintain his attention for only a moment. Then, Will darted forward again, in pursuit of some imaginary storyline.

The trail weaved through the trees and climbed steadily. Ed hadn't recalled such an incline, and he was breathless after the first half hour. A large rock jutted out from the forest floor, and Ed suggested Will play there for a couple minutes while he caught his breath. The boy leaped forward and swung his stick over his head. It landed with a loud crack against the rock and snapped in two. Will mumbled to himself the whole time. Ed could only make out the whispered refrain, "The sword of power is destroyed."

The boy stumbled backward as he played out the scene, but his foot caught a tree root and he fell. Ed moved toward the boy, but Will bolted up. His face was red with rage. "Why is this tree root here!" Will screamed. He attacked the root with his stick, and then turned his rage to the trunk of the nearest tree. It was no longer a game. "Stupid tree!" Will yelled, making animal sounds that echoed across the forest.

Ed watched the boy for a moment, confused about what to do and annoyed that this tantrum had disrupted the forest calm. Will was almost ten years old now; this behavior should've stopped years ago. "Willy!" Ed shouted. Will swirled and landed another angry blow. "Willy! Willy! Knock it off!" Ed had found his way to the boy and grabbed him by the shoulders. Will shrieked. His mouth agape, his teeth barred. Ed matched the boy's rage and screamed, "Stop it."

Silence erupted. The birds were hushed. The breeze halted. To escape the weight of his grandfather's touch, the boy plopped onto the ground. Will breathed through his mouth. "You're too big to act that way, Willy." Ed was angry, and he folded his arms and loomed above the boy.

Will studied the leaves on the ground. The veins were a secret map. He began piecing them together. He wanted to ask to go home. All the way home. Back to Philadelphia. To the forest along the highway. To the hum of his own street. But, his mother had told him to be good.

When he had whispered to her that he didn't want to go, she had said, "This means a lot to Grandpa Ed. Just give it a try. A new adventure. Who knows, maybe you'll even have fun."

He picked up two broad, brown leaves and held them together. A map! The elf had freed himself from the gryphon's claws, survived the fall from the sky, and now, there was a new map. A new path to warn the western troops.

When Will jumped up and lunged forward, Ed stood for a moment in the cold November air and shook his head. The boy acted like nothing had just happened. Not knowing what to say, he reverted to the common denominator. "I'm working up quite an appetite." It hadn't even been an hour yet, but he was thinking that maybe it was time to turn around. Ed *was* hungry, and he was thinking of the turkey and the pies. He thought of the sweet potatoes with marshmallows and the stuffing. He imagined his son-in-law kneading the butter and broth into the dried bread cubes and scooping it into the turkey. He could see Damien's hands—painted nails and wet with the work of cooking—and it turned his stomach. He closed his eyes for a second and breathed in the damp smell of the November woods, and thought of his wife, Belle, and his daughter, Joan. She was home, he thought. For the first time in years, Joan was home for Thanksgiving. And not only Joan, but his two other children and their families—all local to Bradford—would be coming over, and he could imagine the whole post-dinner scene. He would push himself back from the table, and he would update his children on his plans for fixing the roof on the garage. The house would grow colder as night fell, and Ed would show Will how to build a fire in the wood-burning stove. Will would marvel at the glowing coals and the magical warmth. Amidst the wreckage of dinner, the whole family would play Cinch, and his from-somewhere-else son-in-law would be confused by the rules and sit the game out. The grandchildren would get sleepy and doze off watching *The Grinch* in the living room, and Ed and his kids would drink homemade wine, and they would laugh big gut laughs about the one Thanksgiving when it snowed and snowed, and the oven broke halfway through cooking, and they had to pull the cover off the grill and try -- and fail -- to finish the turkey outside.

Ahead, the trail took a sharp turn, and Ed couldn't see much farther along it. Will had run ahead and was out of sight. "Willy!" He yelled. "Wait up, Willy!"

Will darted back into view. He said, "Just here, Grandpa Ed." He waved his arm forward. "It looks really different up here." He was off again, along the trail and out of view.

Ed tried to move quickly, but he could only get himself to half running. Every joint was a bit sore. Even pumping his arms felt like overdoing it. He wondered for a moment how he would ever be able to repair the roof on the garage. After the first snake curve of the trail, it climbed a bit more and then opened into a clearing. Ed saw Will standing on a downed log overlooking the open space. When he got closer, though, he saw that it wasn't just one downed log, but the entire field was a mess of fallen trees. The trail disappeared under the criss-cross of logs. Next to Will, Ed put his hand on the boy's shoulder and breathed. Will studied a large tree that had been pulled up by its roots; no longer hidden underneath the soil, it revealed a network of thick, knotty highways. The entire forest floor was nothing but trees. Why hadn't it been cleared yet? Ed couldn't help but quickly price the trees out for lumber. This could have made someone a fortune. He smiled and said, "How much do you think this is all worth?"

Will was so excited about the maze of logs ahead of him that he didn't even register his grandfather's question. With surprising confidence, the boy jumped from one log to the other. Ed called to him to be careful, to slow down, but Will wasn't listening; he was, by now, a few yards ahead of Ed. "Willy!" Ed yelled. The boy turned for a moment and smiled, then jumped to the next downed tree.

Without the trees overhead, the sun invaded the forest with an eerie brightness and spotlighted the latticework of wood on the ground. Will was back to mumbling to himself, jumping from log to log and hitting his stick against each of the downed trees with increasing force. Ed watched as the boy leaped to a new log, comfortable and confident in his footing. Will's comfort in the forest surprised Ed; he had to admit, a bit sheepishly, that this city kid knew his way around a forest after all. Still, though, he was lost in a daydream; almost ten years old and still lost in a fantasy world, muttering to himself about elves and witches as he bolted from log to log.

Ed waited for Will to turn back toward him. But the boy kept moving forward, further across the mess of timber. Will was already twenty yards away before Ed balanced on the first log at the edge of the path. "I'm coming," he called to Will. The wind was calm but cold, and the sun was bright, if out of place.

Will made it across the trees and stopped at the far edge to look around. "Where's the path?" he yelled back to his grandpa.

Ed planted his feet safely on two logs and tried to remember the curvature of the path. With the trees down, everything looked different, and he couldn't recall what came next. He was sure about a sheer cliff not too far off. And he recalled, maybe, a small clearing with an old oil derrick after that. But did the trail continue north from here, or veer farther east?

Ed looked over his shoulder for the trail marking. He pivoted at his hips, but the move left his feet unstable, and he lost his balance. His right foot slipped from the log and wedged underneath it. He fell backwards, his palms hitting unevenly -- his left on the ground, but his right caught the edge of a broken branch.

The base of his hand sliced open, and blood smeared over his palm. "Goddammit!" Ed shook his hand and tried to untangle himself from the logs. He inspected the cut. It hurt, but it wasn't too serious. He unzipped his coat, untucked his flannel shirt, and pressed his hand into the crumpled fabric. His head throbbed. He breathed deep. He leaned his neck back. It relieved the pressure. A little.

In the sky, Ed noticed a flock of geese. Recently, he had noticed that the flocks he had seen were misshapen. Instead of crisp vees against the blue sky, the flocks Ed had seen were sloppy. At best, they made haphazard U's. This flock was not only late in the season, but they flew in shambles. Shapeless. More a swarm than a flock. Ed squeezed his hand tighter. He wasn't sure if he was angry about the geese, or this failed hike, or his cut hand. He tried to gulp down the anger and turn his attention to the cut. He looked under the flannel and groaned.

Will heard the sound and glided over the logs to his grandfather. "Are you OK?" He asked. He put his hand on Ed's forearm. Ed glanced at the boy's gentle touch and snapped, "You need to stay with me!" Will shrunk back. "You got to learn to listen, Willy!"

Will sat on a log opposite his grandfather. Around him, the forest darkened. The trees sprang back up from the ground. Shadows grew. The space between him and his grandfather became overgrown with thorns and nettles. Will hugged himself. He thought of the word *harvested*.

"Stop that, Willy. Look at me when I'm talking to you." The boy was rocking back and forth now, holding opposite elbows in his hands. He looked everywhere but at Ed. Ed's anger wouldn't be swallowed, so he indulged it. It shocked the boy. Ed pointed skyward with his chin. "Look," he scowled, trying to get the boy back. "Look up Willy!" That got his attention. The boy looked up. "See that. Not even the geese fly in perfect vees anymore."

Will looked up at the geese. "Can we go back?" He felt guilty the moment he said it. Would Grandpa Ed tell his mom?

"Let's just sit a minute." Ed made himself a bit more comfortable on the log. Will watched the geese.

"It should be a perfect vee, to cut down on the wind." Ed tightened his grip on his cut hand and felt his pulse in his palm. He closed his eyes against the throbbing.

Will stood up, still staring at the geese. For a moment, he imagined they were rescuing the elf warrior, carrying him away from the western forces on their backs. The flock dispersed and dive bombed to confuse the gryphon, who was now on the scent of the elf. They were flying south, away from the western forces, in order to buy time. The gryphon tired easily. The geese, however, worked together to cut down on energy, taking turns carrying the elf, synchronizing flight patterns to reduce drag. Ed sucked his teeth and pressed harder on the flannel.

"Can I help?" Will asked, turning back to his grandfather.

"I just need a minute," Ed answered.

Will reached out and touched the flannel that stuck to Ed's palm. "If you want, I can take the pain away." Will pressed his palm firmly into his grandfather's hand. "You just need to push the pain out of your hand." Will looked into his grandfather's eyes. The pressure stung a bit.

"That's all right, Willy," his grandfather said, pulling back his hand and looking away, uncomfortable with the closeness. "That won't help right now."

Will blinked and withdrew his hand. He turned from Ed and looked up. With the trees downed, there was nothing between him and the sky. The geese still hovered above. If they were trying to write a letter, Will couldn't read it. He telescoped his hands and homed in on one of the geese at the head of the flock. He twisted his hands and zoomed in. The gray feathers sprouted like a forest––an entire world soaring in the sky. Will scanned up the body and found the deep black of the eye.

Ed felt a ping of guilt over his outburst. He tried again. "Something must be wrong," he said. Maybe they lost the leader or something." He hoisted himself up and unwrapped his hand. The bleeding had mostly stopped now, but his palm was smeared in the deep red of a dried wound. "They are supposed to be in a V. Like this." He held his hands together.

Will turned to his grandfather and found the V shape through his telescoped hands. He panned up, pausing for a moment at his grandfather's eye: a brown marble hard as a bullet. Then, he scanned up and up into the sky. He found his goose still hovering. He zoomed in again. The black of the goose eye opened like a hole through the sky. It swallowed him whole—every bit. A bright blackness like closing your eyes in the sunlight.

The wind whipped past him. The rhythmic beats of the wings calmed his heartbeat. Will sunk his hands deep into the soft down of the goose's back, and the goose pushed up against his palms, welcoming the caress. The softness felt like relief.

Down below, Will could see his grandfather standing frozen with his hands in a peak. From way up here, the sunlight glistened off the flattened forest. It looked flat and glassy. Will stroked the slender neck of the goose and whispered, *it's not a lake down there. It's just a broken down forest.* The goose honked a *thank you* and twisted its neck to steer the flock away to a more plentiful landing spot. Will thought about staying. He imagined dipping his toes in the cerulean waters of the south and teaching the flock new letters, the whole alphabet, an entire story written in animal bodies in the sky. But he knew he had to stay.

Will fell back to earth, dropping his hands to his side and unclenching his fists, letting the few down feathers float to the ground. He watched as the geese scrawled new letters against the blue as the flock disappeared over the horizon, away from the flattened forest where he stood. He thought, *I hope they find some place soon.* Then, he noticed his own body, touched his belly, and felt a pit growing in his stomach.

"I'm hungry," he said out loud.

Finally, Ed smiled. "You and me both."

Sweet Sparrow

Jordyn-Elizabeth Pimental

Hot to the Touch

Susan Pollet

Does she want to have children
A playground regular asked
As we watched Auntie at the
Playground steering her niece
Away from the scorching hot
Metal on the slide toward the
Water sprinkling from the mouth
Of a cement elephant

Auntie had been through Covid
Twice—smoke-filled skies too often
Planes grounded due to flooding
She kept putting off trying for
Pregnancy she said—not ready
Too much work not feeling it
Job not settled living situation unsure

Lurking in the background of it all was
Auntie's question of how to bring a child into
This world this air this water these challenges
With all these fires and bills and stress
It was not just redirecting offspring away from
Hot slides, too hot to touch
It was how to change the course of everything

Turtle Rock

Karen Colstrom

Private Parties

Robert Harlow

> *The obscene hostess mincing in the hall*
> --Weldon Kees, "The Party"

Is she supposed to be dancing
or cutting something for a pie
no one likes so no one eats?
And how did she get to be,
and how long has she been,
obscene?
And if she is,
then why are we here?
Merely to see how obscene
she can be? And what do we say
to others when they ask,
"Where have you been?"
Do we say, "Mincing in a hall
with an obscene hostess."
Adding, "But it's no one you know,
or would want to know."
And depending upon your need
to be with someone obscene,
you wonder if you'll go back—
that is, assuming you will be asked—
to dance, maybe alone with her
when you find,
after she has welcomed you in
and closed the door behind you,
that you are the one she has chosen
to show, even when she is not dancing,
just how obscene she can be.

Halfway to the Peak

Jordyn-Elizabeth Pimental

The Pond

Galen Cunningham

The willow that hung over the pond is what
I imagine when you say childhood:

Or eating minnows from fish nets, catching
frogs & crawdads, swimming, peeling leeches;

The thrilling fear of a snapping turtle taking
a toe from your submerged feet;

Ice-skating in winter, running the meadow
that sprawled behind it.

Or the quick, caving death—the sudden,
irreversible smothering—I felt when

My father had them fill it with rocks & so
much insoluble earth. He had destroyed

The pond for fear that a child may one day
drown in it—a fair reason I remember

Thinking—& yet, the sinking, the caving in
I felt was not something being saved:

In my heart was the drowning & draining of
the pond.

Ambulatory

Richard Lehan

1.

Gilchrist Manor is my home these days. When I first arrived, they gave me a brochure recounting the history of the Manor. I learned that the original structure dates from the early 1910s when it was known as the Gilchrist Manor for Aged Persons. Ironically, the Manor is within walking distance of the house I lived in for a half century. All those years, I knew it only as the local "retirement home." I never once gave a second thought to the people inside or considered the possibility that I'd end up here one day. That feels like hubris on my part now.

I had been at the Manor for about a month when I told Janine, "I have a new name for this place: *The Glue Factory.*"

Janine is the Nurse Supervisor at the Manor. It would be impolite to ask, but I would guess that she's in her late forties; her short black hair is already flecked with gray. Janine stood behind the counter of the nurses' station while I watched her from a wheelchair on the opposite side of the hallway. In my lap was a pile of recently laundered face cloths that needed folding.

"Why do you say that, Malcom?" she asked me. There was a hint of disappointment in her voice.

"Because the Glue Factory is where old nags like me end up."

"It does you no good to talk like that."

"True," I admitted, "but that's what happens when your prospects for going home are nil."

"We've had this discussion before. Doctor Parvin will not discharge you until you can ambulate safely. You lived alone before coming here, remember?"

"And yet, I'm stuck in this wheelchair growing feebler by the minute."

"Be patient. It takes time for someone your age to recover from hip replacement surgery. Keith is due in on Thursday afternoon for your next PT session."

Janine saw me scowl.

"I know, I know—Keith's a mixed bag." She made a notation on the pad in front of her before adding, "It's his age; he's only one year out of UMass, you know."

"Keith lobbing a beach ball to me with one ear up to the phone is *not* PT, Janine. I need more time on the walker. My body is regressing; I can feel it."

"Well, I can't spare an aide to shadow you while you practice on the walker. Our staffing is down to the bare minimum."

I reached up with the face cloths stacked like pancakes in my hands.

"I'm going to talk to my union steward about all this uncompensated labor I provide, Nurse Supervisor."

Janine took the face cloths from me and smiled indulgently.

"Thank you for helping out with the laundry again, Malcom."

That was how our conversations often ended, with Janine allowing me the small pleasure of teasing her.

2.

I was lucky to have my own room at the Manor but still found it hard to sleep at night. I would lie wide awake on my back for hours inspecting the darkness. Janine would have gladly prescribed me a sleeping pill but I was afraid I'd never wake up again. So, I thought a lot about my wife instead. Evelyn died of pancreatic cancer two years before I broke my hip, and her absence still haunts me. People talk about being haunted by a phantom limb; Evelyn is my phantom beloved. I miss her terribly. Sometimes, to corral my mind, I pray for her; more often than not, I ask her to pray for me.

I couldn't help unwinding the whole catastrophe from beginning to end. Evelyn was 76 at the time; I was about to turn 80. The first thing to understand is that Evelyn wasn't a complainer. It wasn't until I caught her wincing that she admitted that her back had been bothering her. When Evelyn began losing weight, I insisted that she go see Dr. Kim, our primary care physician. But she wavered, attributing the weight loss to an intestinal bug. It finally reached the point where not knowing was worse than her fear of finding out. Dr. Kim ended up referring Evelyn to an oncologist; that's when the dread set in for me. I spent the days before she went in for an MRI researching symptoms of various forms of cancer on the sly. Even so, it was a shock when the oncologist—I've blocked out her name—delivered the diagnosis of pancreatic cancer. Why? Because I knew it was a death sentence.

Outside in the parking lot, Evelyn sat next to me in the passenger seat staring straight ahead.

"I always expected to die in my sleep at a ripe, old age," she murmured, "like both my parents did."

I couldn't make eye contact with her; both hands gripped the steering wheel so tightly it braided my palms.

"A silly wish," she sighed, wiping her eyes with her hands. "At least now I have time to prepare."

After enduring the first few rounds of chemotherapy, Evelyn whispered to me in bed one night, "My only desire is to die a good death."

"What does that mean?" I whispered back with an edge in my voice. "I see no good in it."

"It's means no clinging to life, Malcom, as if I'm afraid of what comes next."

After Evelyn went into hospice care at our home that summer, she would start her day on the cushioned chaise lounge on the back deck. I stood behind the sliding doors as we both watched the birds descend to the feeders in the backyard, then flit away and disappear into the canopy of trees. Evelyn called it her morning prayer sitting.

I ministered to her the best I could, but it didn't come naturally to me. Hospice had set up a hospital bed in the living room. On the night before Evelyn died, I lowered the guardrail on one side, so I could put a clean diaper on her. When I finished, she looked me directly in the eyes. We held each other's gaze in loving silence for a few moments before her eyelids fluttered like she was ready to nod off. The morphine had that effect. I returned the guardrail to the upright position as quietly as I could and let her sleep. At first, that memory was a painful reminder of Evelyn's loss, but since coming to the Manor it has nourished me in mysterious ways. Suffice to say that my Evelyn suffered greatly, but in the end she earned her good death.

3.

"Ok, Malcom, you win." There was a smirk on Keith's face. "Today we'll focus on practicing with a walker."

He began to wheel me down to the rec room for my PT session. One hand pushed me forward in the wheelchair while the other held the walker. It was Keith's way of flexing.

"About time, Keith," I answered.

"That's for me to decide." He was annoyed. "Thank your buddy Janine for putting a bug in my ear."

"Janine is wise beyond her years."

"She's a pain in the ass."

Keith would get over it; the time had come for us to work on my exit strategy.

When we got to the rec room, Keith put the walker in front of my wheelchair and directed me to stand up and take hold of it. I breathed in and pushed off the arm rests on the wheelchair. After a moment of wobbling, my body rose up into a full standing position.

"You look shaky," Keith commented.

"I'm rusty is all."

"Hey, rusty leads to falls; falls break bones."

I kept quiet. Keith continued, "I want you to step forward using your walker. If all goes well, move toward the door. I'll be right behind you, ready to intervene if it looks like you've had enough. The plan is to go out the door and turn into the hallway in the direction of the nurses' station. You can show off for Janine."

"Hah!"

"Ready?"

"I was born ready."

It felt good to stand. Both of my feet were planted firmly on the floor, but I wasn't sure what they would do once I shuffled them forward. I gripped the walker tightly and pushed my left foot ahead a few inches, then did the same with my right foot.

"Eyes up, Malcom. You need to see what's in front of you."

I nodded and took three steps forward this time, counting them out in my head—*one…two…three*—all the while keeping my eyes trained on the door.

"Good. Keep moving."

When I turned through the door, I looked right: the nurses' station was deserted. Keith said in my ear, "See how far you can go, but don't overdo it."

"Roger that."

Walking a step behind me, he added, "Then I'd like to see if you can turn around using your walker and make it back to the rec room to your wheel chair. You think you can do that, Malcom?"

My legs were already weakening.

"I'm about to find out."

"Remember, don't overdo it."

I took several more steps before my legs started rippling in place. Keith appeared beside me.

"Malcom, do you think you can hold on until I can bring the wheelchair to you?"

"Yeah, but my legs may have other ideas."

Keith spied someone at the other end of the hallway.

"Betty!" he called out, "Can you stay with Malcom for a moment? Come quick, please!"

Betty is one of the aides; she immediately sized up the situation and started trotting toward me.

"Look at you, Malcom, out for a stroll!" Her attempt at sounding nonchalant fell flat.

"Thank you, Betty," Keith said. "I'm just going to grab Malcom's wheel chair from the rec room—be right back."

When Keith put the wheel chair behind me, my legs let go as I slid into the seat.

It was time for a reality check. I called over my shoulder, "Good start?"

"You've got a long way to go, brother."

When we got to my room, I asked Keith to leave the walker behind. He put it inside the closet and closed the door. "Keep it there until next week's PT session, okay, Malcom?"

"Ok," I lied.

4.

I practiced on the walker in my room every evening and made incremental progress at first. The nightly exertion and lack of sleep meant napping in my wheel chair for most of the following morning. Janine often nudged me awake when it was time for lunch. But at my next PT session I was able to maneuver with the walker across the rec room and back. The week after, I did a U-turn with the walker in front of the nurses' station while Janine reached out and high-fived me. Keith looked pleased for once.

"You're starting to get your *mojo* back, Malcom."

Even that modest gesture of encouragement fueled my desire to return home. At night, though, I played devil's advocate: What was so enticing about that prospect? Awaiting me was a ramshackle Cape and a fifteen-year-old Honda Civic I didn't have the dexterity to operate safely. Living at the Manor brought me in contact with other people, but I was in constant danger of forfeiting my independence. What I feared most was acquiescing to the institutional pressure to stay confined in a wheelchair. Plus, the longer I stayed at the Manor, the greater the risk of losing the house to pay for my care.

Almost nine weeks had passed since coming to the Manor. My right hip had fully healed, and I had Janine and Keith's permission to ambulate on my own with the walker. After breakfast, I watched everyone in wheel chairs being herded into the rec room to watch daytime TV. That happened to me in my first week here, but after that I refused to go.

"Count me out!" I barked at Janine. Instead, I used the time to practice on my walker, navigating the main hallway for as long as my legs would tolerate. Whenever I needed a break, I retreated to my wheel chair parked against the wall opposite the nurses' station.

That's where Janine was when I approached with the walker from the far end of the hallway where my room is located. She had a tray of Dixie cups in front of her and was filling them with applesauce and pills for the residents parked in the rec room. I made a bee line for my wheelchair and sat down as she finished up.

"Be back in a bit," Janine said as she headed down the hallway with the loaded tray.

I was the only one in the hushed hallway, sunk in a fugue state of sorts. Abruptly, an urgent realization split apart my daydream: *Malcom! You are as ambulatory as you'll ever be; if that doesn't get you discharged, nothing will.*

Now I was anxious for Janine to return. A few minutes later, she emerged from the rec room as my eyes tracked her progress back to the nurses' station. Janine stopped in front of me, her eyes widening.

"It just hit me, Malcom, how few men reside at the Manor."

"Funny, it was the first thing I noticed." I arched an eyebrow. "I like being a unicorn; it adds to my mystique."

Her face creased into a big smile.

That was my cue.

"Janine, I have a request."

"Ok..."

"Can you speak to Dr. Parvin about evaluating me for a discharge home?"

"You think you're ready?" Janine seemed surprised. "Because we've talked about what that entails. Dr. Parvin will review your medical records and consult with me..."

"I can slip you a Benjamin right now," I interrupted.

"and Keith..."

"Damn, Keith will demand twice as much..."

"Be serious, Malcom. Dr. Parvin will also insist that you arrange for at-home elder care services..."

I hadn't thought that far ahead but answered, "If that what it takes."

"Hold on, there's one final test: ambulate with your walker down the entire length of this hallway—that means without falling, of course, but also without getting stuck."

Janine watched me with interest.

"Still want me to set it up with Dr. Parvin?"

"You and Keith have seen me conquer the hallway more than once."

"Yes, but this time Dr. Parvin will be the judge. And he's strict."

"Understood."

Janine had her calendar book out in front of her.

"Keith will need to be there, too, so we're looking at next Thursday at the earliest. After breakfast; that's when Dr. Parvin likes to do these evaluations."

I pretended to flip through my own calendar book.

"That should work; I'll pencil him in."

"You can cancel at any time. But if you're ready to give it a go, then good luck to you, Malcom."

5.

I dreamed of Evelyn on the night before my evaluation by Dr. Parvin. It was a younger, vibrant incarnation of Evelyn who looked upon me with those same tender eyes. I waited for her to speak, but she remained silent and the ambiguity of the encounter unsettled me. At breakfast, I picked at the watery eggs before pushing the plate aside. Still, I was encouraged by how sturdy my legs felt behind the walker on the way back to my room. Janine found me bent over the edge of the bed tying double knots in my clunky shoes.

"Dr. Parvin will be down to see you in a minute, Malcom," she said gently.

"He's late!" I pretended to be grouchy to break the tension.

"Actually, he's on time for once."

"Don't cover for him."

Janine rolled her eyes.

Dr. Parvin and I had met before. With a bulbous head dotted with age spots, he didn't look that much younger than me. We were both old; perhaps that explained our rapport.

Dr. Parvin strode through the door with a thin, red file in his hand.

"You're lost seven pounds since your admission, my friend."

"I miss my home cooking, Doc."

"That's what I'm worried about. Janine and Keith have both told me about your progress on the walker—you can show me yourself in a few minutes. But my real question is this: Are you capable of living independently at home?" He held up the file. "It says here that you have no family support."

"No, but I can count on my next-door neighbors for help." That was not entirely accurate. On one side of me live the O'Tooles, who are of the same generation as me. I used to run errands for them before I broke my hip. The Underwoods are on the other side. Their son Tim mowed my lawn and shoveled the driveway. Terry, his mom, was always there for Evelyn and me; don't ask me about the husband.

"The point is moot is you can't show me you're ambulatory, Malcom."

Dr. Parvin made no effort to disguise his skepticism; our eyes locked.

"*Rise up and face forward!*" I muttered fiercely as I shot up and took hold of the walker in front of me.

That startled him.

"It's Malcom's rallying cry," Janine explained.

Dr. Parvin relaxed. "Alright, Malcom," he instructed, "follow me out into the hallway. Janine and I will walk on ahead to where we can observe you. We'll be joined there by Keith, am I right, Janine?"

Janine had already stepped into the hallway.

"He just waved to me."

"Excellent."

The three of us gathered in the hallway, which was cleared of traffic.

"Now, wait until Janine and I reach the end of the hallway where I will give you the signal to start. Then use your walker to ambulate—*slowly and safely*—to us."

"Be there faster than a postcard mailed from Timbuktu, Doc."

"Take as much time as you need."

I watched their backs recede to the other end of the hallway. They huddled with Keith for a moment and then Dr. Parvin turned and gestured for me to come forward. I looked down at my shoes; the laces were still tightly bound. Objective No. 1 was to reach the nurses' station; if I made it that far, the rest was gravy. In a surge of adrenaline, I made a decisive start; the squeaking of my shoes on the waxed floor was the only sound in the hallway.

Up ahead, Dr. Parvin's arms were folded across his chest, his face a neutral mask. Janine looked relieved, nodding her head to signal encouragement. Keith, my frenemy, was gesturing with both hands to slow down. But I didn't want to slow down; this was my time to shine. After making it past the nurses' station, I actually sped up (relatively speaking). Almost immediately, my clunky shoes started bumping into each other; lightly at first, but then more forcefully. Foolishly, I ignored the warning signs; erasing the distance between me and vindication was paramount.

At the last moment, Keith called out, "Slow down!" and my feet answered by crossing over each other and throwing me to floor. BAM! I landed hard on my left side and yelped in pain.

Keith was the first one to reach me. "Don't move, Malcom."

I positioned one forearm over my eyes to block out the appalling sight of my writhing body.

Dr. Parvin told Janine, "Call an ambulance."

There was a beat of silence before she answered softly, "I think he may have broken the other hip."

6.

It was my first time parked across from the nurses' station since returning from the hospital four days earlier. I spent almost two weeks there recuperating from that second fall—first undergoing surgery to replace a shattered left hip, then recovering from an infection in the surgical area. I left another nine pounds lighter and tattooed with bedsores. The loss of muscle mass meant I needed help getting in and out of the wheel chair. I won't sugar coat it: I returned to the Manor as an invalid.

Janine had stopped by my room earlier in the afternoon with an extra cushion for the wheel chair. I was lying on top of the made bed with my fingers laced together over my chest.

"Will you keep me company for a while?" she asked.

I turned my face away from her.

"Ok, I'll place the cushion in your wheel chair."

Janine waited a moment before stepping away.

"Help me up, please." I sat up awkwardly on the side of the bed as Janine reached out and guided me into the wheel chair.

"Thank you."

"Do you feel a difference with the cushion?"

"Yes."

"I got a pile of napkins that need folding."

"Why not."

Janine pushed me in the wheel chair out into the hallway. We had only seen each other briefly since I got back, and she was making the effort to reconnect. It was my turn to reciprocate.

"I watched TV with the others in the rec room this morning," I said over my shoulder. "Ask me anything about the Kardashians."

She laughed, "That sounds more like the Malcom I know."

"Don't be fooled; I'm running on empty, Nurse Supervisor."

"That's why I want you to start drinking a protein shake with every meal."

"The weight loss is only half the story."

"I understand."

After parking my wheel chair opposite from the nurses' station, Janine brought me a basket filled with freshly laundered napkins. The napkins sat in the basket while I gazed sluggishly at Janine. After a few minutes, she looked up from her paperwork.

"You heard that Keith has moved on?"

"No."

"He decided to go out on his own as a personal trainer. I think he works out his clients at the local Y."

"Godspeed, Keith."

"So, we're still looking for a replacement…"

"That's fine."

I removed a fistful of napkins from the basket and put them on my lap. Just below the surface of my mind, images of the stay at the hospital ran on a loop. For the first few nights, I shared a room with another broken old man, each of us on IVs and fenced in by guardrails. He groaned on and off until dawn while I marinated in self-recrimination. After they moved him out, I found myself with an abundance of solitude. The days pooled into a kind of temporal cul-de-sac that allowed me to contemplate just how impoverished my life had become. There was scant meaning to be retrieved from the wreckage; even my instinct to persevere had frayed thin. Then, surfacing from the deadening, came the realization that I had witnessed this kind of reckoning once before. Except that she had responded to it with more grace and trust than I could muster. But now I turned toward it, fitfully and full of trepidation, but also without looking back. By the time I left the hospital, the dull resignation engulfing me had begun to shape itself into something more rooted and unencumbered.

With effort, I turned away from my thoughts and made eye contact with Janine.

"By the way, I contacted a local realtor to start the process of selling my house."

"Oh."

"How else am I going to pay for my room and board at this swanky joint?" There was no bitterness in my voice.

I began folding the first batch of napkins before continuing, "When the time comes, one of my neighbors is going help with disposing of the contents of the house. I told her to get rid of everything but the photo albums."

"I can help too, Malcom. Your house is right on my way to work."

"No, no—you got too much on your plate, Janine. I'm just letting you know that I'm here for the duration."

Of course, she had already figured that out for herself, but hearing me say it out loud made a difference.

"Not making it home must have been a huge disappointment for you, Malcom, but I'm very glad you'll be staying with us."

"Can't wait to join the rest of the gang in the Alzheimer's Unit in the not too distant future."

"You're sharper than I am, old man."

All the while we were talking, I was taking napkins from the basket and folding and adding them to the stack on my lap. I was down to the last three.

I hesitated and then said, "Anyways, I'm in training again."

"Training? Now, be realistic about walking again, Malcom."

"Not that. Something more demanding."

Janine looked puzzled.

"It's personal; I shouldn't have mentioned it."

"Alright," she said tentatively.

I nodded back at her before reaching out with the stack of napkins cradled in both palms. In the instant before she took them from me, I reminded myself: *Offer it up.*

Sister

Jane Richards

Anne could knit one heck of a sweater,
pink and purple and teal zig-zags,
a little loose at the neckline;
I own it now,
don it on the coldest days.
I can almost sense her fingers in the weave,
the warm imprint of her body.

There are so few photos of her,
no grave to visit, no urn of ashes,
nor tree planted in her honor,
no memorial service pamphlet--
she wanted none of that.

Instead, she is knitted into my life,
her gifts appearing with regularity:
the butterfly pin from Mexico,
a stained recipe for jelly tots,
the commercial grade measuring spoons,
her advice to avoid buying
those dowdy print dresses.

Her loss defies convention,
refuses to sit in its seat,
stay in the cupboard,
be silent.

So like her.

Energy

Clarissa Cervantes

No. 492: A Flamingo's Tale

Brian C. Billings

Lavaca Bay. The gulls and I
have come to terms at last. Goodbye
to Sedgwick County Zoo. I guess I thought
I'd never leave, much less

for land so much like Zanzibar,
whose pools of blue-green algae are
still the waters that I sift in dreams.
The Bay has been my gift.

My place is not in hundreds here.
347, lost last year,
has come again in Carib form—a bird
who did not know the storm

that blew me south on unclipped wings
but comforts me when summer brings
a tempest, and my neck begins to shake.
My mate and I—twins

who did not share a bonding crèche
or capture or enclosure. Fresh
to pairing, faith in me defines his eyes;
their loyalty assigns

to me a deeper role than what
I had allowed—not loner but
commingler. Strain or skim or scoop,
I bend my beak to him.

Painting 3066

Claudio Parentela

Believing Is Seeing

Corinna Underwood

The promise fell from your lips
and landed unbroken on the floor
where we both looked at it,
and wondered who would be first
to pick it up. And I waited
while you sighed, ruffling it
in the current of your breath.
I bent down slowly to look closer
And saw that it was much bigger
than my small, shaking hands,
and perhaps not so fragile.
It did not flinch from my touch.
Your breath held us both
as I raised myself gently upwards,
my arms full of promise
and whispered I believe.
Steadily it rose, into the air
and we could look up now
and see the sky again.

Buckeye in the Prairie Patch

Karen Colstrom

Spirograph

Christine Andersen

As a child,
I placed my sharpened colored pencil
in the center of the smaller circle
that rolled along the ridges of the bigger one.
I made overlapping spheres
that reminded me of the illustrations
I saw in my sister's high school science book.
She tried to tell me about atoms,
but what I couldn't see and touch,
I couldn't believe
and went back to making art,
thinking about the round edges of flowers,
sometimes about a star,
its five points touching the edges
of the little plastic universe
of my pencils.

I grew up to learn that Newton and Einstein
saw patterns in the greater universe.
Newton thought a lesser object
would have a fixed, elliptical orbit
as it circled a larger one,
but Einstein saw a forward-moving,
loop-de-loop dance
like the rosettes I drew with my Spirograph.

Turns out Einstein nailed it.

Mercury does rosettes around the sun.
A star called S2 swirls around the cavernous black hole
at the center of our galaxy in precession
26,000 light years from Earth

where children still sit at their low desks,
selecting a plastic dial and a rim to spin it in,
switching from a red to blue pencil,
unaware that our smallest planet and a faraway star
are dancing the path of their art.

Interior View

Susan Harrison

The venetian blind that covered her sole window was askew. Amelia noticed it as soon as she entered her fourteenth floor Manhattan office. The cleaner must have been in a rush or was not concerned with perfection. But it bothered her, and she knew it would continue to annoy her until she fixed it. On most days, she kept the window covered. The view of the red brick wall of the apartment building on the opposite side of the street didn't tempt her. And even if she had overlooked Central Park, or a Noguchi sculpture, she rarely had the time to look up from her desk. Despite that, she did not lower the blind but raised it.

Across 56th Street, a window, its curtains drawn back, spilled light into the grey flannel air of a January morning and exposed the interior of a room, where a man lay in a semi-prone position in a railed hospital bed. The distance painted the stranger in broad strokes; a bald pate, eyes black smudges against parchment skin, a longish nose, a thin slice of mouth and a chin that disappeared into his neck. For a brief moment, her imagination, and it had to be that, summoned her father's face. Her dad had also lain in a hospital bed by a window, his view a cocktail napkin of St. Augustine grass and a magnolia tree. But today, he was nowhere on this earth. This month made it eleven years since he died in his home in Florida. Eleven years. It seemed impossible she had survived so long without him.

In all her forty-eight years, nobody had told her time dries your tears, but sorrow does not end. Mostly, her father came to her in the form of soothing stories of their shared experiences. But there were times, as in this moment, when his absence coursed through her with the sudden, sharp pain of a paper's edge slicing through skin. In an instant, she was back at his deathbed, the air redolent with disinfectant, her Dad's shallow breaths uneven and barely discernible, her throat dry from trying to voice the right words to pull him from unconsciousness long enough to utter one last expression of love. But God or nature granted them no reprieve and the warm hand she grasped turned cold and stiff.

Caught unprepared by this fragment of memory, Amelia felt a wellspring of sadness rise from deep within her. Even after she turned away from the window, it clung to her. But she had no time to indulge her emotions. Deadlines loomed on several projects, and soon the other attorneys and the persistent ringing of her phone would interrupt her. She shook off her unexpected wistfulness and attacked the tall stack of files and legal memoranda whose demands swept aside the specters of her father and the man in the window.

At 6:30 p.m., she closed her book of Securities and Exchange regulations, placed copies of completed legal memoranda in folders and filed them, put a list of unresolved client questions on the upper right corner of her desk, and closed out her computer. As she sat there, unshielded by her work, the face of the man in the apartment, or was it her father's face, appeared on the window glass next to her reflection. With lifelike stubbornness, this vision refused to leave. It made her dizzy, not physically but mentally. For a while, place and hour were forgotten and her whirling head kept her seated at her desk. Then some internal alarm made her recall her dinner date with her best friend, Heather. Thank God. Her friend would be the perfect antidote to the strange vertigo that had unbalanced her.

Walking into *Oscar's*, Amelia spotted Heather at a booth near the back, a bright parrot among the drab pigeons and sparrows from midtown professional offices. As Heather stood to greet her, Amelia took in her outfit: a lime green floral-print tunic pulled close to her waist by a wide leather belt, baggy navy pants, a large-linked gold chain at her neck, big gold hoops in her ears and chunky, black patent leather boots. She had colored the premature white streak in her brown hair blue, an improvement on the purple shade she'd sported the last time Amelia had seen her. Heather's eyes traveled over Amelia's body as she plopped herself into the seat opposite her.

"Whenever I look at you, I feel like such a failure," Heather said. A frown marred her smooth forehead. "We've known each other, what, almost thirty years, and despite all my efforts, you still dress as if you've arrived to draft my last will and testament."

"That's rather harsh, don't you think? I'm an attorney for a financial services company, while you're a buyer for a chain of chic women's wear boutiques."

"Start a revolution. Explain to those in power a little color and style doesn't affect how your brain functions."

It was an unresolved debate they'd had many times. Amelia had never been able to dissect the thought process of men of a certain age. Years ago, top executives, all male, drafted and distributed a detailed written directive that banned female attire they judged too attention-grabbing for the office. No matter how often HR suggested they amend that part of the job manual to give women more choices, not one letter of it changed. Amelia had been furious at their paternalistic attitude. The executives' fake concern, evidenced by the dress code, was laughable since management looked the other way when a man subjected a woman to a "friendly" hand that slid from shoulder to buttocks of her properly suited and buttoned-up torso.

Until recently, if a woman complained about a man's conduct, he was only given a warning and required to attend sexual harassment training. What a joke!

It was difficult to explain her reality to Heather. Most of the people in her company, including senior management, were women, and so Heather expected the continued advancement of women's equal participation in the workplace, while Amelia was still able to cite examples of subjugation.

"Honestly, Heather, it makes no sense for me to spend energy on a non-starter."

"Okay, you win. I'm too parched to continue this discussion. How about a drink before we order? As I recall, it's the one thing we always agree on."

"Very funny." Amelia smiled at the memory of their early disputes. If Heather hadn't lied on her dormitory questionnaire, they never would have become friends. Because they both asked for a girl who was neat, and an early riser, the college matched them up. It took Amelia less than a week to figure out her new roommate had neither of these traits.

When questioned about the disparity between her housing form and her obvious habits, Heather had been unashamed. "Just because I'm not tidy doesn't mean I don't appreciate a tidy room, and I needed someone who'd wake me up if I slept through my alarm."

They survived their first semester in close quarters because of Heather's unwavering belief they'd be best friends. By then, Amelia had discovered Heather's irresistible sense of fun, generosity, and kindness more than compensated for the attributes that irritated her. They remained roommates throughout college, rented an apartment together in New York City when they started work, and served as each other's maid of honor at their weddings. Years of shared dinners, family trips and incalculable hours on the telephone had created their symbiotic relationship. Amelia told Heather almost everything. Yet, now, she wasn't sure she could disclose her preoccupation with the man she'd observed through her window. It would sound bizarre, and she was afraid Heather would be dismissive. She tried to put him out of her mind and concentrate on what Heather was saying. But the unaccountably familiar man stole her attention and wouldn't be pushed aside. Unrehearsed words tumbled out of Amelia's mouth.

"My father has been on my mind all day."

"Your father was a great guy. He was one of the rare parental types who really got me, you know?"

Amelia laughed. "He always appreciated you. I guess you appealed to his sense of humor."

"It's possible. I'm sure it pleased your father that he's been on your mind."

Amelia tried to keep her expression neutral and resist the impulse to make a pointed comment. Heather not only accepted the existence of heaven and hell but was convinced the departed watched over the living. After death they transformed into personal angels with the ability to read minds and communicate through signs if you were astute enough to interpret them.

Amelia wished she shared her friend's beliefs. It would restore her spirits if she accepted that her father, in whatever form, could read her thoughts and divine the sentiments she'd struggled but failed to voice when he was alive. But this scenario was someone else's fantasy.

"I saw a man today who looked a lot like him. Well, maybe not. It was from a distance, so I might have been mistaken. But I can't seem to get him out of my mind."

Heather's eyebrows went up and her eyes focused on Amelia. There was no laughter or teasing in her voice when she said, "Perhaps your father is trying to send you a message. Have you needed comforting lately?"

"I don't believe in messages from the dead and I've been doing just fine, thank you."

"I know you accept the existence of God which depends solely on faith. Is it such a leap to maintain the souls of the departed can connect with us?"

"It's not the same thing."

"Why, because it was never part of what your parents or your church taught you?"

"There's a limit to what I'll accept without scientific evidence."

"So, you hold that science can solve all the mysteries of the universe?"

"No, I don't think the ability of the human brain stretches that far."

Heather smiled. "That's a big concession for you."

"It's the two glasses of wine talking," she said and then changed the subject. It wasn't until they were pulling on their coats to leave that Heather circled back to Amelia's confession.

"You know, your interest in the man you saw doesn't mean you qualify for a psych exam. I understand I'm not your yardstick for measuring rationality, but to me, your reaction is reasonable."

Amelia thanked Heather with a quick hug. Later, she wondered if Heather's words had given her permission to act uncharacteristically.

In the following days, it became a morning ritual for Amelia to look at the apartment across the way to check on the man in the bed. She would turn off the overhead light and stand so close to the window she could feel the cold radiating off the glass, all to get the best possible view. Amelia made a rule that she would confine her spying to the brief period at the beginning of the day when the office was empty of activity. In this way, she could hold on to the illusion that she was not crazy, merely curious. Then late one afternoon, when the reflection of the sun's rays no longer obscured the interior of the stranger's apartment, she interrupted her work just to stare at him. She strained to see if a visitor had pulled up a chair next to his bed, or if he held a phone up to his ear or worked on a laptop. Any of those activities would have dispelled the concern she felt for him. But he always appeared to be alone, and every day the position of his body changed very little.

Amelia wondered what he contemplated during such enforced inactivity. Was he sick with a survivable disease, or was he dealing with a terminal condition? And if death is your intimate companion, what does your mind latch onto—images of the past, the present moment, or queries about the unknowable future? With her eyes fixed on this stranger, she began to suffer from double vision as her father's face overlapped his, and the present merged with the past.

Twenty-two days before her father died, she had spent a week with him. It was heavy coat and gloves weather in Connecticut, but warm in Naples, Florida, where her parents lived. They had moved after she finished college and left home. Even though she'd visited them many times over the years, she wasn't comfortable in their current place. She forgot where to find tableware or pantry items in the kitchen, and the sofa, chairs and mattress no longer fit the contours of her body. The furnishings of her childhood had been replaced with matching contemporary pieces that always reminded her of a magazine spread or a store display; the wood, glass and fabric surfaces devoid of the scratches, worn spots and stains that once illustrated their family history.

Amelia might have enjoyed the warm weather, but she only went outside once; a trip to the grocery store with her mother. Inside the house, vents spewed conditioned air chilly enough to require a sweater. Beside her parents, the only person she saw was the home health care nurse who came in to help bathe her father and administer medication. Amelia slept in the guest room with her mother who snored loudly from a twin bed a foot away from her own. Late at night, unable to sleep, she went into her parents' bedroom just as she had as a child when she was shaken awake by a bad dream. As soon as the door swung open her Dad's eyes found her.

"I'm sorry did I wake you?"

"No, I was just lying here thinking."

She hoisted herself up onto the hospital bed, eased her weight down on the mattress, and stretched out next to him. His body emanated a cloying floral scent, his breath was fetid and the linens smelled of bleach. Once, her Dad had given off the scent of Old Spice aftershave and peppermint Lifesavers. She closed her eyes and tried to imagine they were back in a time before his illness. But the surrounding darkness worked its way inside her, and she couldn't retrieve that sheltered child. Lying next to him no longer dispelled her fears, as it had so many years ago, it only heightened them. Maybe it was her turn to provide strength and solace.

"A penny for your thoughts" Amelia said, an expression her father always used when he caught her staring into space.

He expelled a breathy chuckle she heard only because she was so close to him.

"Your mother's going to need you when I'm gone."

The response closed Amelia's throat and she had to force out a reassurance. "You don't have to worry; I'll look after her."

Amelia held her breath and waited for him to pursue the subject further, but he was silent. There was still so much to talk about, the provisions of his will, his trepidations and regrets, their shared memories, what his life had meant to him, to her. Amelia's yearning to hear what her father had to say and to respond battled with her disquiet over dealing with such a discussion. She considered picking up the thread of his statement and continuing on, but she held back because he had always been the teacher and she the student, he the leader and she the follower. It was impossible for her to imagine usurping his role, and it seemed particularly cruel to do it now.

The quiet in the room became burdensome. She realized if they were to have this conversation, she would have to initiate it. Unfortunately, she was handicapped by her fear of breaking down and the very traits her father had passed on to her.

Her Dad was not a talker. He had always communicated tenderness or concern by the expression on his face, a hug, driving forty-five minutes to bring her a can of gas when she was stuck on a country road, displaying her report card on the refrigerator, and slipping extra cash in her pocket as she left after a visit. During those nights together, it was her fault they had talked at length about nothing – the weather outside, had she been to the pool, her son's basketball game, the book she was reading, the flowers in her parents' garden, going on and on about unimportant matters. And during those dark hours, what she wanted to say played in a mental loop, background noise to the mundane; "I'm not ready for you to go, You've been the best father in the world, I still need you, I can't manage without you, I love you," but the words remained stored in her head.

The doctors said nobody could predict how many months he had left, and she convinced herself there would be other opportunities to reveal her feelings. If she had known it was the last time they would talk, she might have found a way to express herself. Now, she felt she'd cheated both of them. If she had shared one meaningful thought or emotion, perhaps she would not be left with the loose ends of regret.

January was almost gone. At lunchtime, Amelia left her container of vanilla yogurt and an apple in the break-room refrigerator, walked to *More Than Sandwiches* on 6th Avenue, and picked up a salad. The restaurant wasn't a place she frequented, but to get there she had to walk down 56th Street. On the way back to her office, she halted at the entrance to the old man's apartment building. Movers were carrying in furniture. They had propped both the exterior and interior doors open, and with no hesitation she walked in behind them. One of the workmen held the elevator for her. She accepted the invitation, squeezed in between the wall and a teak buffet, and pushed the button for the fourteenth floor.

There was nothing unique about the empty, beige-carpeted hallway with identical numbered entries on her left and right. The only sign of occupancy was the smell of onion and garlic from someone's cooking. Starting at the hall's near corner, she counted the doors facing 56th Street and tried to figure out which one opened into the room she had viewed from her office. Like the peal of a bell, the phrase "what am I doing here" repeated in her head. Had she developed an unhealthy obsession? The notion made a chill run through her. With quick steps, she rushed to the elevator. As she passed through the lobby, she noticed a bulletin board covered with advertisements and tenant posts. One sheet of paper stood out. Written in elegant long hand, it stated, "Wanted: a bibliophile to read to an older gentleman for forty-five minutes, four days a week." Underneath the job description was the apartment number, 1410, and a request to respond to Arthur Stevenson with his email address.

Amelia was almost positive 1410 was the residence that offered her a view of the man in the hospital bed. She reread the notice, impressed by the fine script and how he had narrowed the field of respondents by using the term bibliophile. Her father had been a voracious reader of novels, biographies, and books on business practices, and they had always traded and discussed books when she visited him. She strained to remember if he read or was read to in his last days. At that moment, her father's end-of-life practices gained exaggerated importance, but her memory failed her. It might be why the simple desire of this Arthur person called out to her. She removed her phone from her purse and snapped a picture of the advertisement.

On the way home on the train, Amelia opened her iPad and struggled to draft a response to Mr. Stevenson's flier. And as she wrote and deleted and rewrote, she found no valid reason to want to read to a stranger, even if he was the man in the window. She wasn't a person who volunteered for organizations that helped others, or someone who had free hours to fill, yet... .

After several attempts she came up with wording stripped down to its essence. "I am a bookworm with good verbal skills and would be available to read Monday through Friday around midday at a mutually agreeable hour." She reviewed her response a few times. She wondered if it would be enough to get her an interview. It was all she wanted, just to meet him. Once she told him her availability would always be subject to unexpected work demands, she was sure he would reject her, and save her from whatever strange impulse had infected her. Yet if that was how she felt, why do it at all? Moments ago, a decision had comforted her, but now her confidence turned to uncertainty. She pulled back the finger poised to hit send and left her reply in her draft file.

When she stepped off the train, the platform was covered with a thin, slick layer of snow and flurries thickened into a fine net curtain. She and her father had loved to walk in the snow the minute a storm ended, particularly if it was early evening when everyone else would be snug inside their houses. Before they ventured outside, they would layer on long underwear, flannel shirts, sweaters, jeans, down jackets, wool knit caps, gloves, scarf, and fleece lined boots. One step beyond the doorway, the cold air slapped them in the face and turned their exhalations into smoke signals. She had loved the contrast between the warmth of her body and her cold cheeks. She and her Dad always held hands; insurance against frostbitten fingers her father would say when she was at an in-between age, and he sensed her hesitation. Before they took their first steps, they looked out over a neighborhood cleansed and softened by the storm. The uneven ground before them was hidden by an unmarked surface of stacked crystals, glittering in the circles of light cast by the streetlamps. Icy air worked its way into any gaps in sleeve cuffs and jacket collars, awakening them from their reverie.

"Let's get moving," her father would say. Tramping into the powder, she and her Dad pretended they were explorers journeying through virgin territory, the dark hollows of their footprints acting as blazes to mark their trail home. Amelia shook her head. Now what had made her remember that? As the snowflakes hit the warm skin of her face, she felt them turn into teardrops.

The next morning, an hour before her alarm was due to buzz, she dreamt she was at the airport about to depart on a flight for a visit with her father. She walked up to the gate for her flight and discovered they'd changed it. She arrived at the new gate and found another gate number posted, and at the next gate the sign board listed a different gate. As her flight's departure time got closer and closer, she became frantic. She continued to run to each location until she woke up in a panic. In the second before she was fully conscious, her belief she'd missed her plane and her chance to be with her Dad made her forlorn. She glanced over at her husband's sleeping form and eased out of bed. Tiptoeing into the next room, she picked up her iPad. With no internal debate over whether her decision was normal or abnormal, she opened her draft email and hit send.

Two days later, Amelia heard from Arthur Stevenson. He asked her to come for an interview the following day at 12:30 p.m. It surprised her because she'd already convinced herself he had rejected her application. The morning of her appointment she found it impossible to focus on anything for more than a few minutes. And when the time came for her interview, she felt as if she had teleported to Mr. Stevenson's doorstep, for she had no memory of the walk from her office to his building.

Now, buzzed in, she hesitated in front of the elevator and gnawed on a fingernail until the coppery taste of blood filled her mouth. An argument in her head grew heated—proceed, don't proceed; sane, insane. She took a deep breath, rode up to the fourteenth floor and knocked on the door to 1410. A male nurse in green scrubs answered the door and escorted her into the living room, which had cream-colored linen wallpaper and a tasteful mix of English and French antiques. An oversized oriental rug in maroon, cream and black almost covered the wood floor. Against the far wall was an enormous mahogany cabinet with beveled glass doors. Behind the panes she saw shelves crowded with books, their multi-colored spines resembling a pop art painting. A man sat in a brown leather, tufted wing-back chair with his legs stretched across a matching ottoman, tasseled loafers on his feet. He wore grey slacks and a glen plaid long-sleeved shirt topped with a charcoal wool vest. A fringe of silvery white hair encircled his bald head.

"You must be Amelia. Thank you for coming. Please make yourself comfortable." He gestured to the chair next to him.

"It's nice to meet you, Mr. Stevenson."

"Please, it's Arthur."

As she settled herself, she glanced at the shadow box end table between them. Bookmarks, expensive by the looks of them, lay on royal blue velvet lining the bottom of the case.

"I see you've noticed my collection of antique silver bookmarks. The oldest is English from the 1860s."

"They're beautiful. Do you ever use them?"

"I used my first acquisition for a while, but once I began a serious collection, I've kept them all under glass and switched to cloth or paper place holders for daily use."

"If you don't mind my asking, which one was your first purchase?"

"The saber in the center. As a child, I loved stories of knights and sword play. My favorite books were *Ivanhoe,* and *King Arthur and His Knights of the Round Table.* I even took up fencing when I was in college, and during my working years I belonged to the New York Fencers Club. I found it helped me in my job as an architect."

"How so?"

"Fencing is often referred to as physical chess for an excellent reason. There is logic and strategic tactics behind each of your moves, and you have to make instantaneous observations of your opponent's physical skills and the psychology of his fencing personality. In a sense, it's not so different from dealing with clients, contractors, and planning commissions."

"That's fascinating. Would I be familiar with any of the buildings you designed?"

"Wait a minute, who's interviewing whom here!" Arthur smiled. "Why don't you tell me a little about yourself?"

When Amelia told Arthur she was an attorney, he nodded.

"Ah, that explains the cross-examination." His dark brown eyes studied her for a moment and then he continued with his questions. Where was she from, was she married, any children, her favorite books, and had she ever read to anyone other than her boys? Then, he had her read a page from a biography, *The Years of Lyndon Johnson.* At home the previous night, she had spent an hour reading aloud for such an eventuality, yet she heard a slight quaver for the first sentence or two before her voice smoothed out. Her desire to be not only passable, but applause-worthy, puzzled Amelia. All Arthur probably wanted was someone with a reasonably clear, pleasant voice that didn't grate on his nerves.

"Very nice. Your verbal skills are as advertised."

Afterward, he proposed a schedule that was good for her with flexibility about arrival times as long as she came earlier than two o'clock. Their conversation had dispelled Amelia's unease, and she found herself drawn to him.

On her second visit to the apartment, Arthur asked her to look through his books and pick out something she'd enjoy. It was a simple task, but it made her tense. For some reason, when in his presence Amelia had a childish urge to please. Would Arthur see her in a particular light based on her choice? This idea of being judged unsettled her.

"I can only guess at what you might be in the mood for or have read in the last year or so. Wouldn't you prefer to choose?"

"Don't worry, I'll tell you if I'm not satisfied with your selection. These days, it's difficult for me to make quick decisions."

His books were familiar to her. Many had had a place on shelves and tables in various rooms of her parents' home. Arrayed in front of her were the works of old companions: Gore Vidal, E.L. Doctorow, John LeCarre, Mary McCarthy, Philip Roth, James Baldwin, John Irving, and Daphne DuMaurier among others. There were also current gems, and a novel she had purchased and loved caught her eye, *A Gentleman in Moscow*. She pulled it out and held it up.

"Have you read this one?"

"I haven't gotten to it yet. It was a gift from my son last Christmas. What's it about?"

"It's set in Russia and begins in 1922, when a Bolshevik tribunal sentences Count Rostov to house arrest for life in Moscow's Metropol Hotel."

The description elicited a laugh from Arthur. It wasn't a feeble laugh, rather the kind that rises above the noise of a crowded room and makes heads turn. And it made Amelia want to join in.

"Well, I suppose I can relate to a person who is unwillingly confined. I'm curious about how someone, even a fictional character, handles such a situation. Your selection is approved. Shall we begin?"

Amelia hadn't read aloud since her two sons were six or seven. She had forgotten how different it was from reading to yourself. She'd never been able to act out the stories the way her father had. She remembered his use of sound effects to imitate a train's whistle, a barking dog or the whooshing of the wind, and how he gave each character a unique voice. Reading to an adult is not the same. Her task was to mind the punctuation in order to maintain the meaning and rhythm the author had established. Sometimes when she glanced up, it surprised her to see Arthur instead of her Dad. Now, his eyelids were closed, and a slight smile pulled up the corners of his mouth. She wondered if the sound of her voice had put him to sleep, but when she paused, Arthur's eyes opened wide.

"Being read to brings me back to my childhood. It's a forgotten pleasure, in the same category as the anticipatory static of a needle on a record before the music begins, or the sensation I get when the nib of a fountain pen forms letters on paper. You know, I really miss the hand-written personal messages I used to receive. These days when you open your mail, there is nothing to look forward to but bills and junk."

"I understand just what you mean, a note or letter was always a wonderful surprise, and it turned an ordinary day into something special. Our mail always came in the afternoon, but I would prolong my anticipation by waiting until after dinner to tear open the envelope."

On the train home, going through her email, she recalled her conversation with Arthur about letters. It reminded her of the last letter she wrote to her father. She and her husband had been about to leave on a trip to Japan and five days prior to their departure date, a Boeing 737 crashed, killing all the passengers. They were scheduled to travel on the same model Boeing. Flying under any circumstances made her anxious, and that evening a nightmare haunted her. In her dream she was on board the plane, her upper body bent over her knees in the brace position, counting the seconds until impact as the aircraft nose-dived toward the Pacific Ocean. Once awake, she was consumed by an urge to update their wills and send a long overdue letter to her Dad.

Amelia's two-page letter included a response to something her father said to her a few months before. She'd been talking about how terrific a friend's husband was with their new baby. He said he was sorry he hadn't been a "liberated" man. It was not something Amelia had ever considered. Her father was no different from her uncles or friends' fathers. Like most men of his generation, his focus was on providing financially for his family. As an insurance salesman he'd spent most of his time with clients, cold calling, or participating in Rotary Club to help increase his client pool and grow his agency. Taking issue with his confession, she reminded him how he had come into her room every night and talked to her before she went to sleep. And he had been very "liberated" when it came to her participation in activities that were considered more typical for males–lawn mowing, baseball, carpentry, and attending law school. She told him how she always felt safe and loved, and how proud she was whenever she glimpsed something of him in herself—her sense of humor, appreciation of nature, and remaining true to her values. Writing the letter was a rare moment when she did not censor her emotions. As soon as the envelope slid down the slot of the mailbox, she wanted to grab it back. Her family, particularly her Dad, avoided sentimentality, and she was uneasy about the contents of her letter. Her father never mentioned it, and she just assumed, with relief, it had gotten lost in the mail. Now she hoped the post office had delivered it.

Four weeks had passed since she'd seen Heather. Her friend's buying trip to Europe had interfered with their usual bi-monthly dinner dates. When Amelia arrived at the restaurant, Heather greeted her with a kiss on both cheeks.

"I see you've brought a bit of Paris culture back with you."

"Mais oui."

Amelia sniffed the air. "You splurged on La Vie Est Belle perfume!"

"A gift from a designer."

"Lucky you."

The waiter asked if they wanted something to drink. Heather chose a dry martini with a twist of lemon, and Amelia decided on a glass of Chardonnay. Recently, she'd concluded Heather ordered a martini because it projected a sophisticated image. She never finished it and when dinner was served would switch to wine.

"So, how was your trip?"

Heather smiled. "It was a very pleasant break. Everyone was so well-mannered, and from a business standpoint, it was very successful. What about you? Any news from the home front?"

Amelia couldn't figure out how to start from the beginning, so she began at a later point. "The man I saw who appeared to look like my father, his name is Arthur Stevenson. I read to him four days a week."

Heather, about to swallow a sip of her drink, choked. "You're reading to your father's doppelganger! How did that happen?"

"Really, Heather? Doppelgangers are a myth. Studies have shown people who claim they've seen a carbon copy either aren't well acquainted with the comparison person or haven't had time to study the look-alike."

"Are you avoiding my question? Tell me everything from the very first day."

Heather's request kicked Amelia back into the morass of her obsessive thoughts and odd actions. But perhaps if she told her story out loud, she could sort through her confusion. Amelia got through the explanation of how she'd stolen into Arthur's apartment building and seen the notice. When she reached the description of their first meeting, her pursuit of a man she'd glimpsed through her window left her perplexed as to her motives. Had she hoped to find someone who was a facsimile of her father?

"When I met Arthur, I saw that any resemblance to my father was a trick of lighting and distance. Other than baldness and perhaps the shape of his mouth, there is no physical similarity. I would guess he's around eighty-three, the same age my father would be had he lived, and he

sounds much the same as my Dad; his choice of words, his references, but that may be generational. It's as if he's a person from my past, an old friend of my parents or a childhood neighbor."

What Amelia said to Heather was accurate but didn't describe how emotional the encounter had been for her.

"Well, that's nice. But why are you doing this?"

Amelia looked down at her hands as if she would find the answer written on her palm. "I don't know why. Do you think I'm being really weird?"

"Weird is our window dresser, Jordan, who's convinced he's the reincarnation of Cleopatra's cat. A cat, for Christ's sake! What's that?! Although, he has the 'no matter what you say I'll do what I want to do so screw you' personality of a cat."

Amelia wondered if Heather was just trying to placate her, but her expression was difficult to read.

"So, as long as I'm compared to Jordan, my behavior will seem perfectly normal?" Amelia couldn't help but laugh, which washed away her concerns. Then the conversational spotlight turned back upon Heather, and she didn't have to deal with the subject for the rest of the evening.

Amelia read to Arthur for two more months. She looked forward to their time together. It gave her the chance to share a book she loved with an appreciative audience, and as the days went by, they also took more frequent breaks to chat. After their first meeting, they never touched on their personal lives. Any mention of background or family was superficial an d secondary to what they were discussing. Of course, they talked about Rostov, the protagonist of the book, and the beautifully fleshed out supporting characters who inhabited Rostov's new world. After she'd read a few chapters, Arthur grumbled that Rostov appeared not to appreciate the fact that his imprisonment did not include solitary confinement. It started Amelia wondering about how much time Arthur spent by himself. Her father was lucky to have plenty of visitors when he was sick. Her parents' circle of friends included people they'd known in Connecticut who had also retired in or around Naples, and long-time neighbors in their complex. One of her father's brothers and his wife also lived about thirty minutes away. She hoped she was not the only one to visit Arthur. She couldn't know for sure without asking, but the question seemed too personal.

Sometimes Amelia and Arthur discussed subjects removed from the topic of the book. He said he enjoyed learning about what the younger generation was thinking and doing in a world increasingly foreign to him. When she mentioned a special exhibition of Impressionists at the Metropolitan she planned on viewing, they found they had a common love of those painters, in particular, Monet, Cezanne and Degas. Amelia told him she'd wouldn't have been familiar with artists and their work if her father hadn't insisted she take an Art Appreciation course her freshman year of college. She was still grateful her father had been so adamant.

She'd never known her father was particularly interested in art, although once or twice during her childhood, her parents dragged her around an art museum. When she associated her Dad with painting, it conjured an image of the familiar planes of his face spattered with her favorite shade of blue. He had spent a Sunday afternoon rolling the color on her bedroom walls after she'd told him she was too old for pink wallpaper with rainbows and purple butterflies.

For two days in the beginning of March, the temperature rose into the high 50's. At lunchtime, coatless people congregated in the streets, and tee-shirted young men on rollerblades and Razor scooters, wove a path between pedestrians, their young bodies on public view for the first time in months. All around her, people exuded a celebratory mood, the weariness of winter put aside and the hope for an early spring palpable.

On the first day of the warm spell, she arrived at Arthur's apartment to find the windows partially opened and an elaborate tea with blueberry scones and lemon pound cake laid out for the two of them.

"What's all this?"

Arthur's cheeks were pink and his grin wide, "I thought we'd have a treat today to usher in Spring."

"You don't suppose it's just a temporary thaw?"

"I've decided to be optimistic."

Amelia wondered if it was more than the weather. Maybe he'd gotten some good news. For a little while her heart lifted. Two days later, a bitter cold wind blew snow through the canyons of the city where it collected in dirty piles in the gutters. Maybe it was a warning that you should never expect too much.

She didn't talk about her friendship with Arthur or her growing unease with anyone but Heather.

It was the kind of story she would have shared with her father if he were alive. From childhood, she had trusted him with her secrets, like the time she was eleven and had whispered in his ear, "I love Joey Benton and he says he loves me."

He had nodded and pantomimed locking his lips and throwing away the key.

At the end of April, the bony scaffolding of Arthur's face and hands became more prominent, and he appeared to have some discomfort. He often shifted his position in his chair and added a pillow behind his back. He also chatted less, letting her read most of the time, and ended their sessions earlier. One Monday morning, she got a call from Arthur's caregiver. He told her Arthur needed to discontinue their visits but wanted her to stop by at noon on Friday for a few minutes.

Amelia's hand shook as she hung up the phone. A shiver ran through her. Now, it was impossible for her to deny what she had suspected from the beginning. Arthur was dying and soon there would be one more void in her life nobody else could fill. Amelia wanted to give him a parting gift, but what do you get for a man who no longer needed possessions. Before catching her commuter train, she walked four blocks in the opposite direction to a stationery store, where she bought a box of paper and envelopes made from heavy cream-colored stock, a Waterman fountain pen, and a package of black ink cartridges. Once home, Amelia retreated to the quiet of her bedroom. In meticulous script, she wrote a well-thought-out thank you, which attempted to convey the immense enjoyment and comfort reading to him had brought her. She ended by telling him, "In the brief time we've spent together, as with the best of artists, you have enlarged my world." Eyes wet, she signed the note, "With deep affection."

On Friday, the walk to Arthur's place went by much too fast. If she searched an entire unabridged dictionary, she would not find the right words to mark the end of their time together.

When she arrived at the apartment, his caregiver let her in and stood with her in the foyer.

Amelia looked into the living room, but her friend was not there.

"Arthur asked me to apologize for him. He planned to say goodbye in person, but he isn't up to it. He told me to give you this," the nurse said. He handed Amelia a small narrow box wrapped in elegant gold paper and tied with a ribbon of deep pink satin.

Amelia thanked him and gave him her note for Arthur. "Please tell him goodbye for me," she said as a film of tears fought to the surface of her eyes despite her best effort to contain them. After the door closed behind her, she stood there for a moment to compose herself before she left the building.

In the privacy of her office, Amelia unwrapped her present. She had hoped there would be a card in the box, but when she opened the lid, all she saw was a layer of pink tissue paper. Underneath it, she found a black velvet pouch. Inside was Arthur's first acquisition to his antique bookmark collection. The sword's silver blade gleamed in the light, and the intricate gothic carving on the hilt amazed her. She placed it in the palm of her hand and stroked the miniature masterpiece with her finger. It was then she understood how superfluous a note from Arthur would have been. His choice of a gift spoke more eloquently than her note.

As Amelia gazed at the sword, she felt sad that her time with Arthur had been so brief, and grateful she'd been allowed her father's company for the most important moments in her life: her graduations, her wedding, and the birth of her children. The memory of her first child's birth surfaced and she was transported back in time. There was her Dad beside her, his arms swaddling his grandson. For a few moments, he stared down at the newborn, and then he looked up and fixed his attention on Amelia, as if he was a compass needle and she was true north. This mental picture made her smile for the first time in days.

The next evening, Amelia lay propped up in bed with her copy of *A Gentleman in Moscow* face down in her lap. Earlier in the day, she'd remembered the box of her father's important papers, still stored in the back of a coat closet at her mother's home in Florida. Amelia considered whether she should visit her. It was possible the letter she'd sent to her Dad so many years ago was among his possessions, providing proof it had been received and read. She pushed her speculation aside for the moment and turned her book over. For the past few months, she had spoken the words aloud and forgotten what it was like to read silently. And it came to her, both methods revealed what the author wanted to convey. Her body softened with contentment. How foolish it was to worry about whether her Dad had received her letter – she had the answer she'd been searching for. Fingering her new bookmark, Amelia decided she'd keep it on her bedside table within arms-reach, in case she needed to mark her place.

What We Leave Behind

Nancy Haskett

After we're gone
there will be baskets of rocks
collected from rivers and shores
across years of travels

unidentified keys
that hang in a closet under the stairs
or hide among mismatched earrings
in a wooden jewelry box,

collections of photos
with people and places
our children won't recognize,
but they will look through some of them,
and our daughter will say,
I remember that dress!
and our son will say,
I learned how to drive a stick shift in that car,
and they will keep just a few
that mean something to them

go through our shoes and clothes,
try on several things,
put some aside for the grandchildren
who have other things to do that day
besides cleaning out the house

but there will be a moment
when they open a kitchen cupboard,
or pull out a drawer,
and some small, insignificant thing
will overwhelm with memories,

and they will laugh
before they start to cry.

Sun's Wrath

Sarah Selim

Chocolate Mayonnaise Cake

Marcia L. Hurlow

--for Jean B. Hurlow, 1927-2018

I want another thick slice of that black-brown cake,
      dissolving batter that stops my voice
      icing stuck around all my molars

Mother made it for me, gave it to me for breakfast
      because I was flying to France for a year

It was the most luminous piece of my favorite cake
      because Mother's tears were swelling,
      because she knew my flight left in four hours

Every crumb and smear of icing made it off
      that white plate, like a full moon over the Atlantic

As I left, the two empty mixing bowls
      huddled in the chipped porcelain sink.

Dusky Iris

Jennifer Weigel

Lost, Chased

Craig Kirchner

I'm ten, dreaming of being chased by
a faceless horror, through
the woodlands of my youth,
where I knew every path and patch,
spending all non-school days
roaming these woods.

There was the need to build a fort,
my space, home, hidden from passers-by,
leery of anyone invading this territory.
I'd fall asleep planning construction,
then dream of running through familiar turf,
from a demon I never saw.

Sixty years later,
I fall asleep planning tomorrow's attempt to
write something meaningful or play golf.
I drive to a pier, get on a small sailboat with friends.
We sail to "Pleasure Island"—
like Pinocchio I wander off and get lost in a
Disney World on steroids.

At each new set the surroundings
seem to be molting.
There are characters that want to do me harm.
I need to get back to the boat,
my friends, be able to find my car,
and now it turns out I don't have the keys.
This bothers me as much as the imminent danger.

I wake as I did as a child, soaked,
with a migraine of fear and my heart pounding,
knowing this is it for the night.
The only difference seems to be the mobility of
the silver Honda Accord,
that has taken me far enough from home,
that there is no fort,
and I have no idea where I am.

Goldfinch in the Pine

Jordyn-Elizabeth Pimental

Beaver Moon

Christine Andersen

Its round silence stuns me.

November's full moon
hovers over the woods
lighting the tips of the bare branches,
floats in the pool
the beavers made with their dam.

In summer we laughed
when a furry twosome
belly-flopped off the bank,
tails slapping the lazy surface
with a splash that rained down
a waterfall of crystals,
bubbles riding expanding circles.
Their merriment was a gift
we carried home.

One late October afternoon,
we watched as a tree was felled,
gnawed at the bottom
to fine points
like the crux of an hourglass—
the beavers with their mounded bodies,
buck teeth and broad tails,
waddling,
hauling and gathering,
layering branches,
preparing for the deep freeze.

When I crawled into bed,
I thought of them laboring
through the night.
I felt a kinship.
Don't we all work to survive?

Under this ripe November moon
the beavers swim into their lodges
built log upon log, stick upon stick.
Settle in.
Savor a hard-won feast.

Painting 1496

Claudio Parentela

The Prayer Girl

David Larsen

Spencer Graell's mother's last words, before she returned upstairs to the adult Sunday school class, were simple and to the point. "Don't get into any trouble. Mind your manners and do what you're told. Then, after Sunday school, we'll stay for the full church service, and the potluck afterwards, whether you like it or not, young man. Do you hear me?"

Spencer was already in Dutch; the last thing he needed was more grief from his mother. He'd caught more than enough hell for talking back to Coach Briggs during P. E. class on Thursday. Spencer was right, of course, but his mother always took the teacher's side, any teacher's, even the dimwit Briggs'. Coach Briggs had no idea what the hell he was talking about when it came to football. The idiot thought the team on offense got the ball after a safety. Duh. Had the coach never heard of a free kick? Spencer had watched the Steelers with his father more than enough—before the man skipped town with a woman ten years younger than Spencer's mother—to know the rulebook backwards and forwards. Coach Briggs was nothing other than a blowhard with a big gut and no brains. His father? Well, he was a man who knew football and baseball, but, unfortunately, was more interested in the women in town, attached or unattached, than any game on television. The laid-off millworker now lived in Erie with some skanky woman his mother refused to talk about, a woman, in Spencer's opinion, not nearly as good looking as the woman his father had left behind.

The claustrophobic room in the basement of the Church of the Redeemer, where the junior- high class met, not only reeked, like a bag of potatoes or even heads of cabbage that had been left unattended for far too long, but was also disgustingly cold and dank, like a dungeon beneath a dark knight's castle in the computer games Spencer played, when his mother wasn't on his case. Unsure of himself, downright ill at ease, and cold, Spencer shivered like a wet pup in January. He should've worn a coat, but coats weren't cool, and, more than anything, Spencer prided himself on being cool.

All Spencer knew was that he definitely didn't belong here. This wasn't *his* church. He didn't *have* a church. He didn't *want* a church. He was here only because his divorced mother was desperate to have a man in her life, any man.

Spencer, one of the "in" kids at Jackson Middle School, had been thrown into this cell of a room all because his mother had recently dredged up a new boyfriend, Larkin Boatwright, a dolt, if ever there was one, and now, come to find out, the cadaverous man with a sinister pencil-thin mustache, a butch haircut that made him look like a goddamned marine and a funky way of dressing—in corduroy, always in corduroy, a corduroy jacket, corduroy pants, hell, probably corduroy underwear—was also some sort of a religious fanatic. Good God, thought Spencer, I'm here only because my mother wants to get laid.

Ten chairs, nine small metal folding chairs with one larger adult-size, drably-upholstered chair, were arranged in a circle in the middle of the room. Each of the tomb's windowless, cinderblock walls was covered with posters of Biblical figures and heroically graphic scenes, several of them portraying gruesome battles, a few of those moderately cool, while others showed an assortment of bearded shepherds holding a lamb, or goat, or whatever. Spencer thought he recognized David, slingshot in hand, taking careful aim at some goon—obviously Goliath—who looked a lot like his mother's brother, Bill, a farmer in the middle of the state, an oaf who raised corn and hogs, a bear of a man who smelled really bad and thought everything, no matter how goofy or silly, was a downright laugh riot. The rest of the figures on the posters could've been anyone from the old days. Saints or angels or whatever.

Seven dweebs, about his age, sat cozily within the circle, each one, with the exception of Spencer, had a Bible in their lap. Spencer recognized three of the girls and two of the boys. They were in his class at school, each of them someone Spencer and his friends mocked as "just another kid from the housing projects", one more of the poorly-dressed urchins with shaggy hair—more than likely teeming with lice—and teeth missing, losers who sat at their own table in the lunchroom and gobbled the lousy cafeteria food like half-starved waifs in the Dickens novel he was forced to read in the seventh grade. No one in class got anything out of the story, no one but Mrs. Stevens, the ancient, diminutive seventh-grade teacher who was thought by everyone, even the dreariest kids in school, to be mildly insane.

Spencer, at times, felt sorry for those kids, the wretched misfits he and his buddies shunned, but not *that* sorry. Not sorry enough to risk his own skillfully-cultivated status in the school. He'd never so much as spoken to any of them out of fear that his cohorts would think him a do-gooder or, even worse, one of the riffraff. Now, damn it, he sat in their midst, when he should be home sleeping or talking to Ben or Shanks on the phone, his own cellphone. He'd bet a dollar to a dime that not one kid in this Sunday School class even owned a cellphone of their own, let alone any cool computer games. And now, here he sat, surrounded by a half dozen of them. They must wonder what a guy of his ilk, one of the neat guys at school, was doing in their hillbilly church. He wondered himself.

A rangy man, dark eyes widely set in an elongated, vitamin-starved, pockmarked face, shambled across the cement floor and sat in the cushioned chair. He looked around the circle like a warden taking count of his inmates. When his eyes set on Spencer, he stopped. His teeth, when he grinned, were as yellow as the trim on the Steelers' uniforms in the fourth quarter of a rough game. The beige, crumpled suit the man wore was badly stained and fit him like a gunny sack. The buttons on his shirt, beneath his wide paisley tie, looked, to Spencer, to be improperly buttoned; there was a gaping hole that exposed a pallid, hairless chest three buttons beneath his alarmingly eager Adam's apple. With something that prominent in the man's throat, Spencer wondered, how does he breathe or, for God's sake, swallow?

"I see we have a new member in our class," said the wisp of a man, apparently pleased with the sound of his bumpkin voice. He grinned and nodded at Spencer. "Would you care to stand up and introduce yourself?"

Each and every damned face in the class turned toward Spencer. He wanted to say, hell no, but he couldn't get away with that. His mother was upstairs doing her best to fit in with these simpletons—all so's some jerk might jump her bones.

Spencer stood. "I'm Spencer Graell." He plopped back onto his chair with a definitive thump.

The Sunday school teacher slowly shook his head. "Spencer, that won't do. That won't do at all. Tell us a little about yourself."

Again, Spencer stood. He gulped, then announced, "I go to Jackson Middle School. I'm in the eighth grade. I played baseball, but I got kicked off of the team." Again, he sat. This time he nodded to the teacher as he slumped defiantly into the uncomfortable chair. He didn't give a damn what any of these yokels thought of him.

"That's much better, Spencer," said the dull-witted man, in an irritatingly nasal twang, like that of some cowboy off in Wyoming or Texas. But this man was no cowboy. Not even close. He was just another rube, probably, like so many men in town, including Spencer's own father, laid off from the paper mill. "I'm Mr. Bandy." He pronounced his name as if it was a challenge. "And I'm certain you know most of the others in the class." Like a serpent with a bad hairpiece the man sneered at each kid in the circle, from one to the next. Spencer expected a two-forked tongue to slither out from between his thin, nervous lips. The Sunday school teacher paused, again grinned at Spencer, then asked the group, "Who would like to lead us in our opening prayer this morning?" He kept his eyes glued on the newest member of the class.

Two of the girls, their lipstick-free mouths zipped tight as a virgin's sleeping bag, the pallor of their skin that of the dough Spencer's grandmother rolled out on her kitchen table before she tossed it into the oven, raised their hands. A little too eagerly, thought Spencer. Show offs. One of the two, Deirdra (Spencer recognized her from his class at school), stood prissily before the other nitwit could take advantage of the opportunity to display her piety.

Deirdra, or was it Denise, bowed her head and began to mumble what Spencer guessed was something she'd learned by rote, complete with a lot of Jesus this and Christ that sprinkled in here and there. Spencer, his teeth clenched so tightly that his jaw ached, studied each kid in the circle, one by one, each listened more intently than the one next to them to every single word the poor girl uttered. Each one as pitifully uncool as the others. A room full of losers.

With a determined, "Amen," the girl finished.

"Spencer," said Mr. Bandy sternly. "In this church we always keep our eyes closed during prayer. It's a matter of paying respect to God." He crinkled his beaked nose, then continued, "In the future it would be best for all of us if you would agree to observe this policy. This *is* the house of the Lord, you know. Could you please bear that in mind?" The man sniffled and began to search for his place in his over-sized, braggingly-bookmarked Bible.

Spencer sighed. "Excuse me, Mr. Bandy. How would you know I had my eyes open? If yours were shut?"

The man glowered at Spencer, then took a deep breath. "I am the leader of this class," he said emphatically. "It's my job to see to it that you learn something about the Bible. It's *your* job to learn exactly *that,* without any attitude. Your mother warned me about you."

Mr. Bandy then commenced to spin a long-winded, yet surprisingly interesting, yarn about Job and all his woes. Spencer had never heard of the beleaguered goof. God seemed to be using the poor slob as a wager in a bet with the devil. Job lost everything, got blisters and was lectured by his friends and neighbors. Spencer thought Job had a legitimate gripe, but, like a wimp, the righteous man didn't so much as utter one word of protest about what had befallen him...all of it at God's whim. Though fascinating, the story still seemed like a crock. This sort of thing didn't happen.

"So," said Mr. Bandy, "what do we learn from this story?"

A boy from school, skinny as a walking stick whittled from a limb of an elm, his hair matted, his freckles about to fully overtake his entire face—a real creep—said smugly, "That we should never question God. That we can't begin to understand God's purposes."

Mr. Bandy nodded approvingly. His Adam's apple bobbed like a yoyo on a string. "Very good, Del. Does anyone else wish to comment?"

The other victims in Mr. Bandy's class looked down at their well-worn shoes, a few mud-splattered work boots, two girls' strapped flats, one pair of boys' gym shoes, a pair of cheap canvas loafers. No one, thought Spencer, has ever heard of shoe polish. Not in this bunch.

Their silence was cowardice.

"Mr. Bandy," said Spencer. The sound of his own voice startled him. "Don't you suppose that Job should've gotten himself a lawyer and sued God?"

The teacher scowled, then said, "I don't think there were lawyers in those days. And, no, we should never question the Lord."

"Says who? It seems to me that Job and God had an understanding. And, for no good reason, God arbitrarily broke his contract with Job."

"Spencer, Job was obedient to God. He would never have done such a thing."

"I would've," said Spencer. He looked around the circle. All eyes were on him. "But, in the end, God backed down and gave poor old Job everything back. Albeit, after he'd put the dude through hell."

The other attendees, their eyes as big as their opened mouths, rustled nervously in their metal chairs. Not at all in support of his position.

Mr. Bandy cleared his throat. The Adam's apple leaped wildly, an animal on a short leash. "Spencer, we don't swear in church."

"Hades?"

The teacher stood, then quickly sat back down. He glared at Spencer. "Why don't you bring our class to an end with a prayer, Spencer.? You seem to have some fascinating ideas. Maybe you can slip some of your superior knowledge into a closing prayer."

All heads bowed, except Mr. Bandy's—his beady eyes remained fixed on Spencer— the room fell silent.

Spencer wanted to show the son of a bitch up, but nothing came to mind. He froze. He hadn't a clue where to begin. He'd never prayed, nor had his mother—as far as he knew—and certainly never his father.

"The devil got your tongue?" asked the teacher.

All heads still lowered, except for Spencer's and Mr. Bandy's (the two sat, eyes wide open, staring the other down), the rest of the class sat through an eternity of awkward stillness. One boy cleared his throat. A girl wiped her nose with the sleeve of her denim blouse.

Finally, Mr. Bandy spoke. "Apparently, our young friend seems to have lost his train of thought." He grimaced at Spencer. "Melissa Ann, would you care to offer a closing prayer?"

A gray-eyed girl, halfway pretty, in a knee-length plaid dress, prayed. A good one, thought Spencer. The little he heard of it. He wasn't really listening. His thoughts centered more on how he could get even with Bandy, the bastard.

An orchestra of clanking and clattering, the classmates, including Spencer, folded their chairs and leaned them against the wall beneath a poster of some bearded old guy with a staff watching soldiers, horses and chariots being flooded by two walls of water. Kind of cool. The geezer, like Spencer, seemed delighted with the spectacle before him.

The others in class, led by Mr. Bandy, clomped, like soldiers off to battle, up the cement steps to the church's sanctuary or whatever the hell it was called. Spencer had made up his mind to hang back; he was in no hurry to join his mother and Larkin Boatwright on a hardwood pew.

"I was glad to see you here today," said a voice behind him.

Spencer jumped. He'd thought that he was rid of the others.

He turned. Melissa Ann, the prayer girl, stood directly behind him, a generous smile on her not-so-plain-as-the-others' face. Spencer detected a pale shade of lipstick on her half-opened lips and a little of whatever girls put on to make their eyes look mysterious. In fact, she looked pretty good, for a nerd.

"I didn't want to be here," said Spencer. "My mother made me come."

"I know. My father told me that you'd be here and that I was to be nice to you." She smiled and swayed dreamily to the music upstairs. "My father's Larkin Boatwright. He's a friend of your mother." She took a deep breath. "I've seen you at Jackson Middle School. I'm in the other eighth-grade class. You hang out with those rough kids, the bigshots." She winced.

Spencer nodded. At which statement? He wasn't sure. "Yeah, I've seen you around school," he lied.

"I'm surprised," said Melissa Ann. "You're always so busy with your friends." She paused. "My father really likes your mother." She clutched her Bible to her chest. "Since my mother died, he's been really down. Then he lost his job."

"I know," said Spencer, perhaps contritely, though that wasn't his intention. "My father, my mother's husband, got laid off also."

Melissa Ann blinked. "I didn't know that your mother is still married. My father said that she's divorced."

"No, they're still married. Happily. He just found a better job over in Erie. He'll come back as soon as he earns enough to finish paying off the mortgage on our house. Then we'll decide, the three of us, whether to sell the house and move to Erie or stay right here." Spencer gathered his wits. He was in over his head. "It all depends."

The girl looked into his eyes. Her lower lip trembled.

"I don't think my father knows about any of this."

"He must."

"No, I don't think he does. He's a bit of a nut when it comes to religion...and doing what's right." Now, she sniffled. Her voice broke. "He wouldn't be seeing a married woman. I'm sure of it."

Spencer looked for the stairs, his escape route. He nibbled at his lower lip, then turned back to the girl. He took a deep breath.

"Not really, Melissa." Spencer shifted his weight. His legs felt like straws. "My father's not coming back. He's got a new woman. But...he really is in Erie."

Melissa Ann shook her head slowly. "Why did you tell me all of that other stuff?"

"Because," Spencer stammered, "I don't like the idea of my mother dating. And, to be honest, I don't much like having to come to this damned church."

She chuckled. "Me neither." She smiled. "I just come because my brother and sister refuse to. I can't stand Mr. Bandy. My father says he's a pretentious fool." She shrugged. "But here I am."

The organ played more forcefully overhead and people began to sing. Not quite a heavenly host.

"I'd better get upstairs or my mother will shoot me," said Spencer. "I really hate all of this."

Again, Melissa Ann nodded.

"I don't think I'll ever come back here." Spencer looked down at his Nike sneakers, his best shoes. "But maybe I'll see you at school." He might. Who can say? He just might look for her. No matter what Shanks and the others thought.

"Are you staying for the potluck?" she asked

Spencer smirked. "I don't think I've got any choice."

The girl stepped back. "I'd like to sit with you and talk," she said, "but my friends wouldn't understand."

"Understand what?"

She slowly shook her head. "Most of my friends don't think much of you or the other boys who hang out and vape and smoke weed on the other side of the fence behind the school. They think you're...stuck up. Or that you think you're better than the rest of us."

We *are* better than the rest of you, thought Spencer. Who the hell do these nerds think they are? Don't they have mirrors in their houses? "No, we don't think that," he said. "We've just known each other since grade school." He wanted to spit. But not in church. Even he knew *that*. "Well, I'll look for you in school. Maybe we could hang out together sometime." Spencer had never had a girlfriend. He wasn't sure how it was done. But the other guys boasted about their experiences with girls. It couldn't be *too* hard.

Melissa Ann shook her head. Her auburn or brown hair fell across her face. "I'd rather you wouldn't. I don't want any of my friends getting the wrong idea." She sighed. "A lot of the kids at school think your friends are just a bunch of losers." Melissa stepped back. "But not you, I think. They'd probably like you...if they got to know you. It just wouldn't be a good idea for me to be seen with you."

Spencer watched the girl climb the stairs with more grace than all of the others combined. Screw you, he thought. Screw all of you.

Shred of Truth

John RC Potter

You said you'd never leave me
not in my prime nor in my youth;
and the greatest lie is one that
still contains a shred of truth.

You said you'd never leave me
and I believed it to be true;
it's true you never left me
but then you made me leave you.

You told me that love doesn't walk away
and there is no mystery without a clue;
but I know promises aren't always kept,
what we've done isn't always what we do.

You said that night you'd always love me
and wanting it I believed it to be true;
it's true you never did stop loving me
but you then made me stop loving you.

Roads Less Traveled

Sarah Selim

An Empty Room

George Freek

I stare at my unmade bed.
Outside, a chilling breeze
rustles the dead leaves.
The moon is a ball of cold lead.
The distant stars, lost,
lost in the infinite sky, don't care.
They have nowhere to abide.
A tattered shirt hanging
from a tree, waves in the breeze
like an abandoned flag,
in a querulous sky.
I feel the approaching cold,
as I watch traffic pass me by,
and suddenly, I know
what it means to grow old.

Peony

Jennifer Weigel

I Wish I Could Stretch the Night Out

Miriam Manglani

like taffy so we could lay in it longer,
a hammock for our naked bodies,
nestled crescent moons.

As the sun rises and spreads
its fingers of light
over a sleepy night,
thoughts of you leaving me
and the warmth we've created
darken the morning.

I run my hands through
your hair where wild fires burn,
stroke your warm dark cheek,
dive into the green pools of your gaze
where I drift in waves.

Between waking and dreaming,
I pull a corner of the night,
stretching it out,
to cradle the infinite stars we create.

Autumn Enchantment

Karen Colstrom

It's in the Cards

John Grey

People I haven't seen in almost forever
still send me Christmas cards,
adding husbands, wives, even children
to the names of the well-wishers
as the years without them
work their way toward half lifetimes.

Here's Lisa in central Iowa,
Nick in Francisco,
Brad and Jenny who love nothing better
than to pepper the snowbound states
with snaps of Arizona cactus
decked out as St Nicholas.

I send my cards in turn, of course—
to some I dearly miss,
to others just a fragment of memory or two
this side of strangers.
I have an address book
that I devoutly reference each December.
I add to the names
but none are ever deleted.
Even as its pages yellow,
it won't let go of anybody.

So every Christmas,
cards go back and forth
across the country,
even the world.

Heart and mind
don't know why we do it
but keeping contact has its reasons.

Succulent

Cheri Williams

Well Water

Kevin McNamara

I was warned about the Reverend during the tail end of my interview.

Mr. Phelps, who ran Phelps Environmental Labs, asked me in a quiet tone, "Are you religious?"

I said, "Not particularly."

He said, "The reason I ask is, on Sunday mornings our lunch room is used by a local minister. Calls himself the Reverend Jim. He's got a congregation of perhaps ten people and since they don't have a church they meet here. We allow them." He coughed into his hand. "Actually, my father allows them. He started Phelps Labs and, since he retired, he has befriended this Reverend Jim. The whole point of me mentioning this is, in the past, there have been some problems with people coming into work on a Sunday, to get caught up or whatever, and running into Reverend Jim."

Phelps stopped talking. Clearly, it was my turn to say something, so what I said was, "You don't like this guy."

"I didn't say that. I just like to give new employees a head's up. He can be a tad overzealous but he's harmless, for the most part," said Phelps.

He asked me when I could start and when I said, "How about Monday?" he frowned and glanced again at my resume.

"You've listed your address as being in New Jersey," he pointed out. We were three hours from that address.

I said, "Oh. I closed on that house last week. I've been staying with my mother in Ithaca." *Please don't ask*, I thought. *You didn't ask me about the cane, so don't ask me about the house.*

He didn't. Phelps was all business, with little in the way of personality, not atypical of your average chemist.

I shook his hand, nodded goodbye to his secretary and limped toward the exit. Phelps Environmental Labs occupied an old elementary school, the classrooms converted to laboratories, meeting rooms, chemical storage and so on. All on one convenient but somewhat claustrophobic level. At least I wouldn't have to deal with stairs.

That weekend, I quickly settled into a small apartment two blocks from the lab, in a sagging Victorian-era house painted an indifferent blue. The tenants of its subdivided interior were all at least thirty years my senior, and generally did not stray beyond their doors. It took me an hour to move my few things from the back of my camper-top truck into my new place.

I did not sleep at all that first night. I still wasn't used to being alone. Part of me still expected one of my kids to come jump on the bed, expected Anne to slip in just as I was falling asleep and put her arm across my chest. Instead, I lay on top of a musty, second-hand futon, massaged my aching hip and watched the trees outside the window cast shadows on the ceiling until the rising sun made them disappear.

Monday, I went to work and met everyone. I was taken out to lunch at a deli down the block by two co-workers named Steve and Lilly, analytical chemists like myself. Both were younger than me, and both were married.

"You married?" Lilly asked.

"I was," I said and let it go at that. They politely did not pursue the topic and neither inquired about my cane.

The rest of the week I settled into a routine, and became familiar with my equipment, my surroundings. I was in charge of three aging, battered gas chromatograph / mass spectrometers, machines that analyzed samples that had been extracted from soil or water for the presence of certain chemicals deemed harmful by the Environmental Protection Agency. The machines did all the work. I fed them samples, maintained their overly delicate parts, and ran the data they produced through a computer. I was nothing special, a facilitator, a technician. It was exactly what I wanted.

Blissful anonymity.

I did not have anyone over to the apartment. I did not go out for drinks with the gang from work or attend their barbecues or softball games. The word quickly spread that I was anti-social. I did nothing to counter these opinions. I went to work, performed my job, and limped home. I ate all my meals in the tiny kitchen of my apartment and at night, I would hobble around the streets of Hamilton, New York.

I could forget that I used to have a different life.

I could forget I had once had a family.

I could forget quite a lot.

Fifty emergency samples arrived one Friday afternoon a few months into my tenure. They were from the site of a tanker truck accident on the interstate up near Syracuse. Thousands of gallons of toluene had spilled near a creek. The soil into which all of this solvent had soaked needed to be removed. The only way to know if all the solvent had been recovered was to analyze the surrounding soil. The New York Department of Environment Control used a backhoe to dig up tons of earth. Soil samples were taken, placed into glass jars, labeled, boxed, and shipped to Phelps Labs.

The DEC wanted the answers ASAP.

I worked late into Friday night, loading all three machines at once and letting them run continuously. Saturday, I came into the lab and re-loaded fresh samples, compiled data, analyzed the results, and let the machines run overnight again.

Sunday morning. Tired but oddly invigorated, I woke at six, went for a short stumble around the block before the heat of the July day kicked in, showered and walked under the shade of very old maple trees to Phelps Labs. Four cars were in the parking lot at this hour and I attributed them to other chemists handling the same workload as I was.

I had forgotten all about the Reverend Jim.

I punched in my access code next to a door that had decades ago opened every morning for children. I thought about those children once in a while, now adults, with presumably an adult curiosity about their past. How many of them had driven by, perhaps in anticipation of pointing out to their own kids the very school they had attended in their youth, only to find that the building had been transformed, with odd stainless-steel chimneys poking out of the roof, into a laboratory?

Inside, I heard guitar music and singing. I stopped in the lobby. The music was coming from the lunchroom to my left.

The lunch tables had been folded and pushed to one side. In their place were rows of folding wooden chairs, all empty save for a handful at the front. One of the lunch tables was converted into an altar of sorts, bearing a large wooden crucifix, candles, and other assorted church items. A short man in a blue coat stood behind the table, strumming a guitar and leading his tiny flock at the top of his voice.

Jesus the water of life will give,
Freely, freely, freely;

Come to that fountain, oh drink, and live!
Freely, freely, freely.”

They were really into the hymn, standing and swaying with their arms in the air. The singing man, who must have been the infamous Reverend Jim, spied me loitering in the doorway and brought the performance to a clanging halt.

"Brother!" he cried in a near-desperate tone. "Welcome! Please come in."

Oh, shit, I said to myself and raised my hands defensively. "Sorry, just looking." I almost ran down the hall to my lab at the far end of the building and by the time I got to the door to my lab the music had started up again.

I am not religious. That there was no benevolent god in charge of everything I took as an obvious given. This had been my position from high school until I was married and remained my position even after I had killed my family. Especially after.

I had been drunk. As was Anne. We weren't usually drunk. We drank socially. We were, however, *very* social. Even with two kids, we still made it to quite a few parties, dinners, get-togethers. In fact, now that we had two kids, we went to more parties than ever, usually bringing them along because all of our new friends had kids as well.

We lived in northern New Jersey. I worked for a pharmaceutical company famous for its television ads promoting pills for erectile dysfunction, while Anne worked for another pharmaceutical company five miles down the road. I was a chemist; she was in marketing. We had a very nice house.

On July 4th, we were at the Henderson's place for a pool party. They had three kids, two of which attended the same school as our own. They also had a keg of beer sitting in a plastic wading pool of ice and a folding table loaded with gin, tequila, vodka and rum. By the time the fireworks began to rise over the trees, I could hardly walk.

Anne, who had been working on vodka tonics all afternoon, did not try to stop me from getting behind the wheel of our minivan. Kyle and Bethany were in the back. They made sure to buckle up, just like we had taught them. They were ten and eight.

We saw ourselves as smart, respectable parents, firmly ensconced in the upper middle class, living the Dream. The kids were clean and healthy and bright.

I ran a stoplight a half-mile from home. An SUV T-boned us from the right. I woke up in the hospital, under arrest. My hip was shattered but I was alive.

A nurse told me that I had killed my family. She looked at me as if I was nothing much to look at.

I wasn't.

Sunday morning turned into Sunday afternoon. The machines hummed away. I thought about getting a sandwich.

Someone knocked at the entrance to my lab. The Reverend Jim stood in the doorway. He was smaller, it seemed, than when I had first seen him in the lunchroom. Perhaps the guitar had made him look bigger. He wore a dark blue coat and a tie over an orangish shirt. The tie was black with a white cross on it. He also wore cowboy boots and black polyester pants.

"Hi, there," he said. "May I come in?"

"I guess." I was in front of GC number two, doing a bit of maintenance on it, reattaching the ultra-delicate glass tubing lined with silica through which the vaporized samples flowed. It was tricky work because the tubing had to be cut evenly at the entrance point, otherwise the sample would not enter properly and the whole run had to be cancelled. I did not need an interruption, especially from a minister. I should have said no. I don't know why I said yes.

He took a few careful steps into the room, glancing around him at the tools of science, his face neutral. He looked as if he wanted to fondle a cowboy hat but all he had were his own hands, which worked slowly and methodically at one another.

He said, "My name is Jim Jones. Reverend Jim Jones."

I slowly turned toward him. "You're kidding."

"It is unfortunate but there you are. My mother named me as I am. I minister the Church of the Good Word."

"Yes, I saw you in action as I came in this morning."

The Reverend smiled. He sat down in a drab green industrial metal chair by the side of my desk. I had to look over my shoulder at him while I put GC number two back together. He said, "We do like our music."

I nodded. GC tubing is scored with the straight edge of a hard tab of plastic, then is bent until it snaps. My scoring was not going well. All my snaps were angled, unusable. I was getting frustrated.

I said, "So what can I do for you, Jim?"

He said, "Not a thing. Just came down to say howdy, maybe I can do something for you. You're new here? At the lab?"

I nodded, scored, bent. Angled again, but less so. I tried again, and said, "What can you do for me?"

"I can offer you the cup of eternal salvation, for starters."

"Not interested. I just had some coffee. Thanks anyway."

He ignored my sarcasm. "Are you already affiliated with a particular church?"

"I am an atheist, Jim." I turned and looked right at him so he would get the point. The next step would be to ask him to leave but his diminutive size, his polite manner, the look of hope he wore on his face all stopped me from being rude. Rude but perfectly within my rights as an employee. Mr. Phelps had made a point of telling me that I was not to tolerate any proselytizing from the Reverend Jim. There had been trouble in the past. Bibles had been left on lab benches and desks. Machines had been prayed over. Only the intervention of Mr. Phelps's aging father had kept the Reverend from finding himself without a meeting place.

The Reverend stood, as if it pained him. He said, "Well, I am sorry to hear that you are an unbeliever. But I must say I am not surprised." He put a hand on my arm, gently. "Nothing personal, my friend. Only that it's slim pickings with you science types. Your minds, your hearts are shut to God."

"Sorry to disappoint you."

"Oh, you don't disappoint me. I'm merely a messenger. You got to worry about the man upstairs." At this point, he looked as if he wanted to put that imaginary cowboy hat on his head and hitch up his pants, ride off into the sacramental sunset with a couple of crosses in his holster and the Good Book in his saddlebag. I might have told him to shove it, had I been in another place, another time, as another person.

Now, I said, "I don't believe there is any man upstairs, Jim. So I'm not interested in attending your service. I liked your guitar playing, though."

He smiled. He looked genuinely pleased. "Really? I got to tell you, I have been struggling with that thing for going on ten years now and I just recently felt that maybe I was starting to get a good hold on her."

"You play anything besides gospel?" I scored, bent, snapped, and was rewarded with a perfect edge. I slipped the end of the tubing into the fitting in the oven of the machine and began to tighten the screw.

He said, "Indeed, I do. I play a few tunes by Roy Acuff. You like country music?"

"Sorry. Strike two."

"Dang." He laughed and crossed out of the room. "Have a good day, friend. Perhaps we'll talk again."

I waved. I told myself I would never work Sunday morning again.

Yet the image of the Reverend stayed in my mind. I almost could think of nothing else. The walk back to my apartment along empty sunken sidewalks was usually agreeable but that evening any pleasure I might have taken in lilac bushes or mossy lawns was ruined by this sudden obsession, this mental talisman of the Reverend Jim. He was there as I entered the hot apartment; he was there while I made a sandwich and ate it at my table. What was it about this little man that made him stick in my memory, made me want to revisit him again and again?

I tried to watch television, but the Reverend nodded at me. The phantom cowboy hat persisted in being held between his hands. I walked around the block, but the Reverend walked with me. Finally, I lay down on my futon in the oven-air of the bedroom and forced my attention onto a science fiction novel, *Gateway*, by Frederick Pohl. An asteroid is discovered which holds a pathway to the far reaches of the galaxy. I was gone. The Reverend remained on Earth. I was in the heavens, on strange planets, orbiting the furious energy around a black hole.

Some hours later, around midnight, I emerged only because of thirst. I drank water over the bathroom sink and the Reverend smiled grimly back at me in the mirror. He looked tired. Lost.

That was why he had been on my mind. I knew that look. I knew that look intimately.

I stood over Kyle's body wrapped in the firm embrace of the coffin. Bethany's coffin remained sealed, as did Anne's. There had been too much damage.

Kyle looked unscathed, although very pale, very still. I touched his cheek with the back of my fingers. I couldn't cry anymore – my well of tears had dried up.

On crutches, I finally turned away and sat in the front row of a church I had never been in, next to my mother who wept continuously. Across the aisle sat Anne's family. Her father looked as if he wanted to punch me, or worse.

Prayers were said, not by me. The rituals were performed, the end was reached, and I dumbly followed the three black coffins down the central aisle past hundreds of strangers, drawn to tragedy as a dog is drawn, by scent, to the rotting animal carcass in the woods.

And then I smiled at all of them, thanked them for coming, began to shake everyone's hand that I could manage, faint as I felt, yet oddly, terribly happy, because I knew, suddenly, that none of this could possibly be real, that I was trapped in a vodka-induced coma or maybe I had come down with meningitis and my body was sucking air from a machine at the Bergen County Hospital but soon the medicines would work, soon I would awaken and see Anne happily bent over me, cooling my forehead with a cloth.

So I decided to enjoy myself and by the time I got to the stairs at the front of the church I had angered half of the attendees. Someone stepped forward, someone did throw that punch, but I was reasonably sure that it wasn't Anne's seventy-year-old father because the blow when it came was solid and harsh and knocked me off the steps, breaking my collarbone, destroying the idea that my current reality was false.

It was all too true.

I naturally thought of killing myself. Impulsively at first, then, as the weeks following the accident congealed into one amorphous mass of slow time, and as I healed in spite of myself, I found the idea of suicide to be an interesting problem. The options were many: quick or slow, painful or likely not so painful.

I was released from my job at the pharmaceutical company. *Fired* was too impolite a word for the company. I was let go, like a gasping fish hauled ashore, contemplated over and thrown back into the cold water. This prompted me to run from New Jersey. I sold the house to a couple from North Carolina, the first ones to make an offer. I sold every item in the house that I associated with my family, leaving me two suitcases of clothes and my books. Family albums full of pictures I burned as a final act in the empty house's chimney the night before I left. I sat on the bare living room floor and burned it all, every last smile and birthday cake and bike ride and kiss.

My father's shotgun, an inheritance, leaned casually in the corner and as the last lick of flame curled the last picture edge, I grasped the stock of the gun and sat on the fireplace ledge and pressed the cold holes against my throat. My right hand reached down and found the trigger, my thumb easily rested on it. I closed my eyes and sat there for many minutes.

I left the shotgun, still loaded, on the floor in front of the fireplace. I could only imagine the reactions of the house's new owners when they arrived the next morning to commence ownership, and saw the shotgun, and the mass of ash in the dead fireplace. A helpful note to them could have read: "Dear Mr. And Mrs. Whatever, Here are the remains of the Weston family, a loaded gun, its potential never put to proper use because of the cowardice of Mr. Weston, and in the fireplace all that is left of the recorded memories of his family, whom, during one night of entirely thoughtless and self-centered action, he killed as quickly as one puts a key into the lock of one's new home and enters. One out, one in. This is your caution. Remember this shotgun, these ashes. This is what happens when a family is destroyed. Beware."

The summer continued. Construction projects, reclamation projects, accidental spills all kept me very busy. Consequently, I found myself coming into work one Sunday after another, despite my vow to the contrary.

The Reverend kept his distance, confining himself to his end of the building, his small group of believers. One Monday morning I arrived at the lab to find a cheap, black and white tract sitting on the writing pad of my desk. It was entitled *The Devil and Charles Darwin*. The lurid details within portrayed a positively deranged Darwin, bug-eyed and drooling, out to destroy religion with his crack-pot theory that we were 'the cousins of monkeys.' I supposed this was the Reverend's not-too-subtle way of expressing his disapproval of me, atheist scientist that I was.

The following Sunday I happened to run into him coming out of the building as I was coming in.

"Leaving already?" I asked.

He looked angry, the imaginary cowboy hat in his hands a misshapen lump. He said, "My flock is experiencing a momentary, uh, miscommunication. Seems they're all at another service this morning. Seems they think that meeting here in the bosom of secularist evil ain't a good idea."

"Secularist evil?"

The Reverend grimaced with what might have been embarrassment. "Those are Carl Dickinson's words. Bearded fellow, wears a lot of black? I love him dearly, but he's got some ideas that even I think he too ardently champions."

I said, "He's the one who put that pamphlet on my desk?"

The Reverend sighed. "That was him, no doubt. I'll talk to him. Mr. Phelps told us we're not to do that, otherwise we'd be shown the door. I wasn't aware Carl was lurking down that way."

I was oddly relieved that it had not been the Reverend.

I saw less of him the following month, although I was still working those Sundays. The money was nice, the time away from myself even better.

My body was healing but I was not. I did not expect to heal. I almost did not want it to happen. An open, self-inflicted wound was a fine thing to prod. A hobby, of sorts.

And then one day I saw the Reverend on the street, down by the deli I frequented. He was walking to his car, a battered brown wreck.

He said, "Didn't know you lived round here."

"Up the block. Getting lunch?" I indicated the bag sagging in his hands.

"Not for me, the missus. She's got intestinal troubles but swears the only thing she can keep down is a meatball sub from Lou's here."

"They are good," I said. The Reverend looked somewhat bent as he stood by his car, as if something was pressing down on his spine. A gold crucifix dangled from the car's rear-view mirror. Various pamphlets littered the front seat and dash.

He said, "Can I ask you a question? I mean, I know you're an atheist and all but I'm curious."

"Sure."

"You ever read the Bible?"

"What, all of it?"

"Any of it."

"Yeah, when I was a kid, you know, in church and stuff. Sunday school."

"But you ain't never seriously just sat yourself down and studied that sucker from stem to stern?"

I said, "I never had any reason to."

"Because you don't believe in God."

"Pretty much."

"Something happen to you? Something bad? Recent? You mind me asking? Made you turn your back on the Lord? I notice you use a cane."

"I'd made my mind up about the Lord long before…" I trailed off, a lump in my throat. In all this time, I had not said two words to anyone about the death of my family. The words did not exist.

The Reverend said, "What happened?" His voice had lost its pulpit-authority, and we were just two men, talking on a street corner.

I said, "I'll see you around, Reverend." I turned back home, away from the deli, no longer hungry.

Behind me, he said, "There is solace in the Lord, my friend. There is comfort."

My feet ceased to walk, and I felt burning blood creep up my neck, around my ears. I swiveled, as best I could on my ruined hip. It was lucky that the Reverend, clutching his plastic bag, hunched over in his cowboy boots and bloody-Jesus necktie, was not within arm's reach, for if he had been, I sincerely believe that I would have grabbed him and tossed him through the plate glass window of the deli.

Instead, I finally said the unsayable, in a rush, the words spewing from me like lava from a volcano, like vileness from the devil himself. I forget, actually, the specific words, the sentences I used. Hardly matters. The details were there, the horror, the guilt. The raw essence of my tragedy delivered to his cringing ears, on this hot, bland mid-afternoon in front of a mediocre deli in a mediocre town in upstate New York. I did not hold back. I let him have it with both barrels, as it were.

When I was finished, when I could say no more but simply stand there panting with anger and grief, it was not I who began to cry but the Reverend Jim. Twin tears tracked down the sides of his nose, dripped onto the bag in his hands.

He said nothing. He nodded slowly, almost to himself, but he was looking at me, as if I had just appeared out of thin air. He got slowly into his car and drove off.

Sunday, back in the lab, September now, a chill in the morning air.

I had not seen the Reverend in well over a month.

Gas chromatographs three and four had to be shut down during that week due to problems with their injection ports. These were old machines, ten years out of date, with a lot of miles on them. Small labs like Phelps relied on rebuilt, used equipment in order to compete with bigger, better financed companies. It was simply part of my job to be constantly tinkering and fixing tired, balky machines but it took time and sample logs were backing up. I had to work the weekend again.

This time, I slipped in through a side entrance and avoided the lunchroom. However, either the Reverend had a sixth sense, or he just liked making the rounds of the building. Around noon, he stood in my doorway once more.

He looked drained of blood and small dark bags hung under his eyes. He did not knock. He said hello and sat down in the green chair.

I said, "Going to try again?" I was at the desk, processing data on the computer, so I had a level eye with him, although I did not much look at him, steeling myself for another round of Jesus talk, promising myself that I would be polite this time. Patient. He ran a hand over his face.

He said, "No. Not today. I wanted to ask you a question. A science question."

"Oh. Go ahead."

"You test water here, right?"

"We can."

"Well water?"

"Certainly."

He pulled a small vial of water from the pocket of his jacket and handed it to me.

"Would you mind testing that for me?"

I said, "I would love to but the problem is, there isn't enough here. You need a bigger sample size, about five hundred milliliters." I leaned over and from a pile next to the desk plucked a blue-topped sample jar. "Here. Fill this up and get it back to me. I'll take care of it."

"Do I pay you?"

A good question. "Usually, billing is handled by the people in the office, so I'll ask them tomorrow. Do you suspect something is wrong with your water?"

The Reverend Jim Jones did not say anything for a long moment, as he sat hunched beside me and rubbed at his chin, staring at the tips of his cowboy boots.

He said, "I don't know. I suspect my faith is being tested."

"Alright."

The Reverend's eyes were dark, dry marbles. The skin on his forehead seemed fragile and thin, as if I could reach across the desk and pinch a spot just above his eyebrows and start pulling off his shell. The fluorescent lights of the laboratory were blunt, unforgiving, exposing this suffering man.

He said, "My wife. Stomach cancer. This is her second bout. And me, well, I got it the other end. Colon. Just found out a couple days ago."

"I'm sorry."

"This could be my test, you know. Like Abraham's. A test of my faith." His words were not the sure-flowing stream of assurance I usually heard from the other end of the hallway but came haltingly, as if he was choking on them.

I said, "I see" and the hollow politeness of the remark must have jarred his ear.

He said, "You know, it's a funny thing. Most of my associates, friends, family, they're all good Christians. They're all solid believers in the goodness of the Lord. These are people I talk with and work with seven days a week and despite the size of my congregation they keep me busy. I don't have much time or call to socialize with people like you. Unbelievers. I got to remind myself that there are many of you in the world, just as deserving of God's love, if only you'd open your eyes and see. Don't take this the wrong way, I mean no disrespect, but sometimes it seems to me that you all ain't quite...real. That living in the shadow as you do makes you just another temptation, another stone on the clean path to righteousness. It is an odd feeling to have, when talking to another human being."

I said, "I'm one of God's little tests, huh?"

"Maybe you are and maybe you ain't," he said, waggling his hand. "Just the way I see things sometimes. I meant no offense."

"None taken. But you still haven't answered my question about your well water. If God is testing you with cancer, why are you suspicious of your water?"

The Reverend sank back into himself. He said, "We live out on an old farmstead up on Route 13. Lots of springs in the area so we make do with the shallow well that's been there since who-knows-when. Never had a deep one dug, never had the need. Got a piece of plywood across the top of it. I never put on anything permanent because every year I got to do down in her to clean out the end of the intake valve for the pump. Anyway, so's it's real easy to pull up that plywood and get at the water. And from what my neighbors are now telling me," he said, as if his neighbors rarely had anything to say to him, "the guy who owned the place before us used to dump all sorts of things down in that well. Wasn't too firm in the head. Thought it was a sort of garbage disposal."

"Garbage would have mostly just decomposed," I said.

"Yeah, but someone caught him pouring motor oil down it once. Said he did it all the time. Changed his own motor oil, didn't know what to do with it, threw it down the well and then said, it kept the pump running better. Can you imagine that? The ideas that people get in their thick skulls?"

"I can believe it."

"Upshot is, Susie's got cancer, I got it, now what? I can't sue anyone, not that it'd do any good anyway, the guy sold us the place died years ago."

"Well," I said carefully. "It seems to me you have your answer already. Why waste money on a test?"

He said, "Because maybe, just maybe, that water is clean. As clean and pure as spring water can be. I sure as hell never tasted nothing wrong with it and neither did Susie. So I got to thinking. If it is clean, then *this* is the test. The Lord's test. Testing my faith in him."

The Reverend Jim licked his lips, as if he was very hungry and a thick steak had just been passed under his nose. He was not looking at me. His admission hung in the air of the laboratory like an embarrassing fart. He needed, yearned, for a test of this magnitude (and double doses of intestinal cancer are not insignificant tests). Clean well water would be a confirmation of his belief. Cancer did not just spring up out of nowhere. It, like the rest of creation, surely had a cause. And what greater cause than the Lord Himself?

I said, "I'll be happy to test it for you." He promised to bring in a proper-sized sample on Monday and, after slowly rising from the chair, staggered back down the hallway to his tiny flock.

The following Sunday morning, I woke rested. I was just starting to think I might be human again. Ever since my sidewalk confession, nightmares no longer trailed me down into the recesses of my sleep. I tried not to credit Reverend Jim's tears too much — all he had done was listened.

But maybe that had been enough.

I showered in the coffin-sized stall of my tiny bathroom. As I drank coffee and ate toast in the kitchenette, I could feel the heat of an Indian summer sun already baking through the roof over me. I was glad for the air-conditioning of the lab, for I was headed back into work once again, but not to catch up on any tasks or last-minute samples.

The sun was bright and the trees over the sidewalk seemed to bend a bit under its solid glow.

I let myself into the laboratory building. The Reverend Jim was not singing this morning. I turned left and a few steps brought me to the entrance of the ersatz church. He sat silently, head bowed, on a folding chair, surrounded closely by his tiny congregants, who also held their heads low in obvious quiet prayer. I silently backed away and waited for him in my lab.

The wait was not long. My computer had just hummed to life when he tapped at the doorway and walked in.

The week had eaten at him. The cancer, I guessed, was spreading fast. He had not divulged the prognosis, but I could clearly see that things were not going well.

He did not sit as so much fall into the chair by the desk. He threw a grim smile my way.

"Well?" he said.

I couldn't let him suffer anymore. "Clean as a whistle. As pure as spring water can be."

He smiled. His eyes, previously dull with pain and the knowledge of the end, gained some life. He shook my hand and, leaning to me conspiratorially, said, "I knew it. I just knew it."

He paused at the door. "God works mysteriously, does he not? That you, my kind atheist friend, would be the bearer of this good news."

"It is strange," I confirmed.

"Not strange. Just mysterious. God Bless."

He left.

I made sure that the actual results of the test I had run were deleted from my computer. All the raw data from the GC/MS was sent to electronic heaven.

The routine paperwork I had generated for billing purposes I then gathered and shredded in a machine in an office down the hall. The Reverend was not going to be charged. I hoped he would never ponder why he had not been sent a bill.

Finally, the remaining amount of sample sitting in a refrigerator in the extraction lab I poured into a waste can, then threw away the glass container.

While I performed this final act of deletion, I made sure that I wore protective latex gloves. The Reverend Jim's well water was pure poison.

Three weeks later, I heard about his death from one of the church members. "He went quick at the end," he told me, shaking his head. "But he was happy. 'I'm going to see my father,' he kept saying. The faith that man had."

His wife Susie, however, rallied and wound up moving to Ohio to be close to her sister. Their house went on the market that November. I drove out there one Saturday morning and was shocked at the bucolic scene that greeted me – for some reason, I'd had an image of the Reverend Jim's property as a ramshackle mess. I guess I had confused the man with his ideas.

The two-story house sat on a slight rise about two hundred feet from the road and was surrounded by twenty-two acres of woods and fields carefully kept mown. A small pond teemed with sunfish, small mouth bass and frogs. Despite its age, the weather-beaten barn had a good roof and foundation, as did the house it sat behind. Jim and Susie had obviously loved the place.

The following Monday I offered the real estate agent exactly what Susie was asking and took possession by the end of the month. The first thing I did was hire a contractor to fill the old shallow well with cement, which raised a few eyebrows but since I was paying no one said boo. Then I got a professional crew to drill a much deeper well on the other side of the property before the frost set in.

The water it produces is delicious and as clean as water can be.

Some nights I sit on the front porch, bundled up against the sharp winter air, and sip that ice-cold water while marveling at the brilliant wash of stars I never saw when I lived in New Jersey. I think about my family and how much I miss them. Then I think about starting a new one and filling up the empty house behind me.

Feeling Blue

Clarissa Cervantes

The Waif

John Grey

She steals underwear
at the Target store,
is always ready to run
if spotted.

Her shoes are worn,
feet callused,
but her legs are strong
from being poor.

The lake is
where she examines her spoils,
sits on the bank
where boys fish,
both black and white,
examines her haul.

"Is there something here
I can wear?
What about the color?
Maybe this will fit
my baby sister."

Yesterday,
it was cheap jewelry.
The day before,
packs of food —
just add water.

So many stores.
So little money.
So much to run from.

Swedish Country Charm

Karen Colstrom

Tomorrow's Grasses

Buff Whitman-Bradley

Two horses are grazing
In a broad field of winter grasses.
One of the horses is a chestnut
The other is dark brown.
They are standing far apart
From each other.
The air is cold and damp.
The sky is growing dark.
Neither horse seems in a hurry
To finish eating
And head back to the stables
At the close of day.
The trees at the edge of the field
Have lost all their leaves.
With their limbs bared
They look quite formidable.
They might be sentries
Guarding a nighttime bivouac
Making certain no unwanted intruders
Cross the perimeter.
The horses seem to trust them
To be vigilant
Allowing them to continue grazing
Without fear of interruption
By coyotes or wolves.
Soon it will be completely night.
The difference in color
Of the two horses
Is gradually disappearing.
They will become dusky shapes
Walking slowly through the darkness
To their stalls
Where they will spend the chilly night
Bedded in new straw
Listening to the quiet talk of owls,
And the midnight whisperings
Of tomorrow's tender grasses.

Monarch in Flora

Karen Colstrom

Streetlights

Hannah Woodvine

hopeful, I walk towards home once more,
enticed by the gilding glow of the town lights:
lurid with a rose-tinted sheen.

tentatively, my footsteps follow the familiar cobbled road
under the gaze of a newly gouged hole
where the light of the moon once was, should be.

undeterred, my thoughts dress the ghosts in optimistic veneer,
hold onto the hope that a home warmly waits,
unchanged with open arms, as before.

As I trudge past tombstone houses, the streetlights sour,
sneer. They flicker a hollow, pretending glow, casting this place
in the shadow of false embers, the grave

of the place I came from. Its bereft face stares blankly
through gouged sockets, pallid and stiff: gutted.
I commit my hope to the ground. And I leave the ghosts to their streetlit

shadows, content to roam the cobbled roads in darkness.

Jim Bird

Robert McMichael

What Jim didn't know, and what Nelson didn't want to tell him, was that his father and grandfather were dead.

As they neared Pukatawagan, Nelson sighed. "I had no idea how far in the bush you're from," he said. Jim kept his gaze focused forward. "Well, I doubt they'll go to the trouble of looking for you, anyways. It's too damned far, even if the ice road stays good." Jim kept silent. "I get why you don't say much, seeing all there is to look at here. Maybe Puk is way different…"

Jim wasn't sure if Nelson was being sarcastic. The ice road was the only way by car to get to Pukatawagan. You can see the road by air during the summer, and it's interrupted by every lake possible, going into the south end and out of the north end, and then only a short distance on solid ground before entering another body of water. Iced-up lakes make good, flat roads, but are only safe to drive in January, February, and part of March, most years. The rest of the year, the road is mud and heavily potholed. The only sizeable travelers on it the short time during the year that it lacks snow are moose and deer and wolves, and maybe one or two people who live in the bush away from everything. Nelson had never been on this road, and liked the challenge of finding a new route somewhere.

Nelson was a distant cousin of Jim's who worked for a bootlegger and game-buyer in Winnipeg who knew a few residents east of Pukatawagan, near Nelson House, who had a ton of moose meat they wanted to sell cheap. Nelson volunteered for the long drive, even after learning about the detour he'd have to take to bring Jim back home. The Ford F100 pickup truck's heater barely worked, so the two young men were bundled up against the cold: blankets, a couple of old bear skins, beanies, and mittens. The din of the ice spraying up against the truck made it hard to converse or even think, and the endless hours matched the endless bush tundra. Nelson's boss knew of the Bird family, that they were known to be good hunters, and told Nelson he'd let him keep any profits from any game he could buy from them, which is why he volunteered to kidnap Jim from Guy Hill School, which even Cree in Winnipeg knew was the school they built in Manitoba to replace Sturgeon Landing after it burned down in 1952. Some thought a student did it, at least that's what some thought.

The kidnapping actually wasn't that hard. Once Nelson learned through the family grapevine that the Birds had said they wanted Jim back from the school, he was at the Guy Hill School at Clearwater Lake with the truck within two days. He'd gotten word through another cousin which dorm and bunk Jim was in, and at 2 a.m. he jimmied a window in that building and crept up to his sleeping cousin, and – after a tense information exchange – swept him out of there and into the truck.

Jim's brain whirled. He hadn't been home in eight years. He was about to turn 15 and wasn't sure what home would look like or who would be there still. He'd only gotten a few letters in the first couple of years and was not allowed to reply to them. Guy Hill School allowed parents to visit their children twice a year, and to take them home for the summer, at their expense, but Jim's family didn't have the money for the travel, partly because the only way to get there cheaply – by car – was in January or February when the ice road was passable. The rest of the year, the only way in or out was by train or plane, and both cost too much. So he'd given up on them, as he thought they had on him, and he was dulled by the anger until he willed it away. He'd learned enough at school to fit in and get by, enduring the beatings and staying alive while other children disappeared regularly with no trace, and he watched schoolmates go home for the summer and come back in the fall and seem happy aside from the beatings and strict rules stripping hair and language and other Indian things from them. He felt different from them but tried to deny to himself that he was jealous, or that it had something to do with his family. He'd felt guilty for several years whenever he remembered he'd forgotten all his Cree, and before too much longer he knew he needed to let that go, too. Once he stopped trying to imagine talking to his grandfather – what he'd say about the porcupine he watched from his window late at night when everyone else was asleep, how he'd interpret the bear Jim kept seeing in his dreams – the guilt faded away. The dullness set in. But as they got closer to Puk, Jim felt himself looking forward to seeing his grandfather, and started feeling nervous about how much he could show him he remembered.

The familiarity of Guy Hill, Jim began to realize, had lulled him into that dull acceptance of his fate. He started to realize fate might not be right, or that there might not be any such thing. Nelson knew that Jim's uncle and a couple older cousins still lived in Puk, and expected they'd have meat to sell. It didn't make sense to tell Jim about his father and grandfather; he'd find out soon enough.

When they got to Puk just before dark, Jim was surprised he remembered the way to his house. He directed Nelson to it, but immediately noticed, even in the winter twilight, how run down it was. Paint was all but gone from the plywood walls, and the metal sheets on the roof had come undone in places, letting the weather in at the edges. Browned ice lined the crumbling foundation. A light in a window and a thin veil of smoke from the rusted stove pipe deflected the gloom a little and told him someone was home. Butterflies.

Nelson turned off the motor, and they both got out and walked to the door. Jim's mother opened it. She smiled, gasped, and then grabbed him around the neck. "Ki sākihitin," she said. She said it again. Jim did not understand. He began to cry. "I love you," she said.

His grandmother watched from the corner of the room, half in the dark. He could see her watching, blank-faced. In another chair across the table from his grandmother, a young girl who looked like him stared, but he didn't recognize her. In the far corner of the small room, near the door to the back room sat his uncle, whose mustache now had a little gray in it. His face, too, lacked expression.

Nelson moved into the open from behind Jim and said, "Tānsi." The others returned his greeting. Then the only sound the wood burning in the stove.

Jim's mother clung to Jim's arm and said something in Cree to the others. It sounded harsh, but Jim didn't understand it. His mother knew so, and whispered in his ear, "I said they would make their own dinner from now on if they weren't nice to you."

Jim dreamed that night of a word he heard over and over again in his grandfather's voice. "Papêtikwâskopaniow." When he woke, he asked his mother what it meant. She didn't know. He went over and asked his grandmother. She looked at him suddenly, directly, and responded in Cree. He didn't understand and looked at his mother.

"She wants to know why you are asking about this, where you heard it, how you know it," Jim's mother said.

"I dreamed it last night."

His mother spoke to her mother in Cree, and the old woman responded. Jim's mother translated: "She says you are bad news, bringing your grandfather from his rest. That is his word. She said, 'You don't know Cree and aren't Cree and Cree words do not belong in your mouth.' I am sorry she's so cranky."

"I just want to know what it means," Jim repeated.

His mother spoke again to her mother, more emphatically this time. The old woman folded her arms, pursed her lips, and looked down at her lap. His mother softened her tone and moved closer to Jim's grandmother. Finally, the old woman spoke in Cree. Her daughter translated.

"She says it means the thundering sound a grouse or ptarmigan makes with its wings when it takes off to save its life."

Jim's grandmother spoke again. His mother translated: "She says she had a grandson once who especially liked trapping partridges, and was good at it, showed respect for the birds' lives, and his grandfather gave him the name Pinêw Nâpêšis, Partridge Boy." Jim's mother laughed.

Jim faintly remembered trapping ptarmigan and spruce grouse in the snow with his grandfather but couldn't get the memories to come as thickly as his dream. His grandmother considered him dead. Language. And whose fault was it? *They* let him go. He remembered clearly the day the white men took him and his twin brother John away. He could have had no idea this is what it would lead to. If his grandmother only knew what he'd been through. Maybe she did. Maybe that's why she was acting this way. He had thought everyone would be happy and relieved he was home finally, even though his brother wasn't with him. Did they blame him for John's death? Did the school ever tell them about it? He felt he was being punished for being punished for eight years. He went outside to find Nelson.

Jim's cousin, Randall, and Nelson were in a shed talking about moose hunting. "Your cousin doesn't have any moose to sell me," Nelson said to Jim. "They only have enough, maybe not even enough, to get through winter."

Jim asked Randall who was left in the family to hunt beside himself. Randall ignored him. Nelson answered for him: "Just Randall. Everyone else is dead or gone."

"I can hunt," Jim said. Randall scoffed and left the shed. "Why is he being such an asshole?" Jim asked Nelson.

"They all blame you for not protecting John, and for forgetting your Cree. And for cutting off your braids."

"I didn't cut them."

"You know what I mean."

"Does my mom feel like they do, too?"

Nelson thought for a second, then said, "Yes, but she's your mother, so she might be able to forgive you in time. She told me all this last night after you went to sleep."

Jim felt like he was floating when he needed to be on land. Anger came to him. He pictured the bare dirt surrounded by snow behind the boiler room at school, where the children's bodies – including John's – lay. And now, finally, he'd returned and they didn't want him. Even his mom.

"When are you going to get that moose?" Jim asked.

"In the morning," Nelson said.

"Can I come with you?"

"Sure. I could use some help, and they don't seem to really want you here. It would probably be okay in a while once they got used to you being back, though. Your call."

"I'm going with you," Jim said.

They left early in the morning without waking or saying goodbye to anyone. It was a long drive, about 12 hours, and they didn't say much to each other, except when there was a close call with a moose on the icy roads. After a couple of near misses, Nelson said, "Damn! We could fill the truck with those two and not have to drive all the way up to Nelson House, and not have to pay for meat, either!"

Jim said, "As long as the truck didn't get totaled."

"Oh, yeah, good thinking," Nelson said. "I heard moose management was a problem up here but didn't really know." Then another couple of hours of icy tire spray white noise.

They stopped for gas at Cranberry Portage and refilled the emergency 5-gallon gas jug they'd emptied on the way to Puk. Nelson came back with a few sticks of hard jerky and offered some to Jim. That kept them both busy chewing for a while. More white miles passed.

Once in Nelson House, it was all business and Nelson got it done quickly, buying the already-skinned moose quarters from his acquaintances, loading it in the pickup bed, tarping and tying it down, and giving them the cash for it. The rear end of the pickup sagged under the weight, and Jim noticed one of the rear tires was nearly bald. The sellers offered them a bowl of stew and some bannock and they ate it quickly, then filled the gas tank and empty containers at the service station in town, and then began the day-long drive back to Winnipeg.

Nelson noticed Jim was sleeping and thought about what he'd do with him. He thought about telling him to get out at the next town they went through and try to get back to his family in Puk. He knew Jim wouldn't want to do that, and he didn't really want to force him out. But he wasn't sure what he could do for him in Winnipeg. They hadn't talked about that at all. Jim, as far as Nelson knew, had no family there, and Nelson didn't have any extra room at his place, which he shared with a cousin and his uncle and his uncle's wife. But he felt sorry for Jim, too, and knew he couldn't fend for himself. Jim wasn't annoying like a lot of kids his age, Nelson had noticed. He was easygoing and kind of thoughtful. But there was also a sadness and a kind of passivity that followed Jim around like a wake from a slowly paddled canoe. It wasn't severe, not enough to rock things, but definitely there. Nelson had heard about John, but never knew him, and he wondered if losing a twin sibling was different than losing another kind of family member. Or maybe, Nelson thought, Jim was just a sad guy and always had been.

Soon Jim woke up when the pickup blasted through a deep pothole. "Rise and shine, chippy!" Nelson said, smiling.

"Huh? What's a chippy?"

"Nothing, just something my uncle says."

Jim looked out the window at the black and white blur.

"We gotta talk about what's gonna happen when we get to Winnipeg," Nelson said.

"Yeah."

Jim worked in Winnipeg and stayed with Nelson and his family for almost four years, until just after his 18th birthday. It was cramped in the two-bedroom apartment, and Jim slept on a cot in Nelson's room. Everyone was nice to him, and treated him like he belonged. Nelson's uncle, Bill, drank too much sometimes, but wasn't a mean drunk, and didn't disappear for long when he went on a bender. Maybe a couple of days at most. Nelson's aunt, Sherlene, cooked better than anyone Jim knew, and hardly said anything ever, except to make fun of Bill's subtle lisp.

Most of the work was hard physical labor, mostly low-skill construction, but Jim picked up a lot of skills just by watching and was a quick study. His favorite thing to watch was welding, so he took his breaks whenever he could near anyone running a welder. Nelson kept an eye out for Jim at first, letting him know who to work with and who to stay away from until Jim developed his own city sense, which didn't take long. The weeks went by. Years. It was calm. He wasn't really happy but wasn't sad, either. It was. There was lots of luck. Some weekends in winter they'd drive north an hour or two out of the city and find some geese to shoot. And once a year they'd do a long drive to buy moose from up north. But they never returned to Pukatawagan. Jim was okay with that but wasn't sure if Nelson or his folks were trying to protect him from something.

Sherlene insisted on Sunday dinners. It was her church, the family and the food. Bill presided, and there were usually a few other extended family members there, as well. Their dining table couldn't handle everyone usually, but they improvised and the kitchen counters, table, and the top of a short bookshelf would be covered with food. All made by Sherlene. Sherlene also insisted that the Sunday meal be alcohol-free. Despite this rule, it was always well-attended. Over

the years, it had become clear that the main reason for its regularity, aside from the delicious food, was the event's dryness. In the early days, before her decree, the meal would almost always end in bloodshed of some kind.

One Sunday before Jim left them, Bill was telling his usual stories about family escapades, accompanied by lots of eye-rolling and guffaws, and a few shouts of encouragement. Everyone knew Bill liked to tell stories and took most of them with a sizeable salt grain. Although she didn't ever tell anyone, Sherlene found Bill's exaggerations and improvisations historically inaccurate and therefore unpleasant. She disapproved, but rationalized this by telling herself that it was a small price to pay for the institution. And she was proud of it, especially that it was one of the only affairs she knew of in her community that prohibited booze. As Bill continued weaving his tall tales to most everyone's delight, Sherlene – making an exception to her habit of non-participation – interrupted Bill.

"Tell the one about Big Bear and his Swampy Cree wife and son," she said.

Bill's face dropped. The room got silent. "I can't tell that one here," Bill said.

"Why not? You tell all kinds of other stories. That's the best, even though…"

"Woman, don't make me do that. Jim's here," Bill said.

"He can handle it," Sherlene said. "Look at him. He's waiting." Jim looked back and forth between Sherlene and Bill, wondering. But didn't say anything.

"Jim, I gotta do this," Bill said. "She's ordering me to, and you know what that means, right?" Most of the others laughed. Someone spilled a glass of punch. "And you gotta know I don't mean nothing by it, it's just what happened, or what some people say happened."

Jim blanched. Nelson sat next to Jim and whispered something in his ear, smiling. Jim turned to him, eyes pretty wide.

Bill continued. "Okay. A long time ago, maybe almost a hundred years back, there was this bad-ass Cree chief called Big Bear. You can read about him if you want. *Mistahi-maskwa.* He lived most of his life over in western Saskatchewan, near Jackfish Lake. But he *loved* to go hunting. He'd hunt anything, and usually killed more than his share. His father taught him, and when he was a kid he got more successful than his dad or any of the elders. They said it was because he talked to the animals' spirits. He knew them, and was friendly with them, and spoke their languages. All of them. Birds. Moose. Rabbits. Foxes. Even wolves. They would talk with him, ask him questions about what he did with their fur, their bones, their teeth, their feathers. But not the bear. Yes, he would talk to the bear, but mostly he listened. He never killed the bear. You know that. You know why. And he did what the bear said. Usually, the bear would give him tips on where the other animals would give themselves up to him. But sometimes, not often but really occasionally, you know, the bear would give him some bad news. Bear would say that because so-and-so in his village pissed off the wolf by trapping it and not killing it well, and not skinning it and using it right, and not eating it, there would be a price for that, which was that the hunters in his village wouldn't see any game for a while. Maybe you jackasses should think about that the next time you get skunked, eh?" Everyone but Sherlene laughed. "Sorry, Sher, for the bad word," Bill said.

"Anyways," Bill continued, "eventually the curse would break, and they'd start killing animals again. Some hungry days, yeah? But things would even out, as long as they respected the animals good." Someone choked on potato salad. "Anyways, Big Bear was also a warrior and feared a long way off. Nobody picked a fight with Big Bear unless they wanted to die. And they knew they would, too. One time someone picked a fight with him and won, but that's a different story I won't go into now."

Sherlene passed more food around. Bill continued, "So you know what kind of man Big Bear was. Well, maybe you wouldn't think he was the kind of man who would cheat at anything, on account of how respectful he was to the animals. But you see, he did that so he could get what he wanted, and usually that was game, stuff to feed himself and his family. But he also wanted the ladies, uh huh." Bill smiled suggestively, and everyone groaned. He went on. "Big Bear had a bunch of 'wives,' and by that you should know he got around a bit. He was known by the white man as a nomadic hunter, but he was known also by his own people as a nomadic fucker!"

Sherlene cast an icy glance at Bill and scowled.

"You asked for it, girl, you're gonna get it," Bill said. "Anyways, Big Bear had a big appetite, and that resulted in a big number of kids. One of those kids became known later as Bad Bear, and it's said that Bad Bear's mom was Swampy Cree, from way up north, north of The Pas, near Pukatawagan!"

Everyone looked at Jim, who looked confused. "Do I gotta spell it out for you, nephew?" Bill said. "See, Bad Bear – who the books call 'Little Bear' – is the *known* one from the Swampy Cree woman, but the truth is that there was another boy, a *twin*, that she kept *with* her. Big Bear wanted to take both with him, but she wouldn't let him. If you know Swampy Cree women, you can understand this. Stubborn. Mean, even. Not like Sherlene."

A few people laughed. Sherlene smiled.

"Anyways, she kept the one twin," Bill said. "And that twin was a Bird. Ol' Jim here, he doesn't know this, but he came from this Bird. Which came from the Big Bear. And these two Bears, Big Bear and Bad Bear, ended up down in Montana after the Rebellion of 1885. They fled Canada and ended up on the Rocky Boy Reservation, yeah, they call 'em 'reservations' there, not 'reserves,' don't know why, but anyways that's where they ended up. And they both had a bunch more kids. So Jim, you didn't know this, but you got blood down there in Montana."

Jim still looked confused, and focused on the food left on his plate.

"Now here's where the story gets interesting," Bill continued. "When that Bird who was half Bear was about 20 he got a girl pregnant and they got married, and she had twins, too. Two more Birds with Bear blood. One of them would be Jim's great grandfather, who he never met because he died in a hunting accident before Jim was born. Nicked his femoral artery field-dressing a moose and bled to death without knowing he was even bleeding. No sh… No BS. The other twin left the bush around Puk and went to Montana to look for his relatives on the Rocky Boy Reservation. They said he left because he was sick of the mosquitoes up there in the swamp. The funny thing is that he got malaria pretty soon after getting to Montana. Anyways, he found the Bears, and wanted to change his name from Bird to Bear but they wouldn't let him. They said he was from the swamp, so he had to keep the Bird name. They really didn't want anything to do with him."

"Get to the good part, Bill!" Sherlene said.

"Okay, okay. So this Bird was at Rocky Boy and he was mad they wouldn't let him become a Bear, so he tried to poison Bad Bear, but not before sleeping with Bad Bear's wife. She got pregnant with his child, somebody caught him putting something in Bad Bear's food, told Bad Bear, and Bad Bear just came straight at him and cut him open without saying anything. Bad Bear had heard Bird'd been with his wife and was already thinking of killing him, but this just quickened the deal. So they refer to him as Bad Bird, and if you hear any stories about Bad Bird, you know Jim comes from that blood since he was the twin of Jim's great grandfather. Most of the people in Puk know this story but don't like to tell it, first, because it's nasty and, second, because it happened in Montana and not Canada. Too much baggage. They, we, we all, already have too much baggage. And too much moose meat, right!? Eat up!"

Jim was glad Bill was done telling the story. He felt the looks of everyone. He finished his plate of food and dropped the paper plate and napkin in the garbage and put his fork and knife into the kitchen sink, despite Sherlene telling him to just leave it on the table. He came back to the table for his cup, refilled it with punch from the half-gallon pitcher and poured a little 7-Up into it. There was an empty chair in the corner of the living room, and he went to sit. On the couch next to Jim's chair, another uncle, Bill's brother Carlton, visiting from Calgary, sat and patted his belly as Jim sat down. "*Tansi*, Young Jim! Good food, in'it? I might burst," Carlton said. "Some story about your family, in'it? Pretty odd stuff. Ever been to Montana?"

Jim didn't really know what to say, so he just said, "No."

"I been once, years ago, can't even remember when that was. We went for a 'landless Native' pow-wow. There was all kinds of Indians there: Blackfoot (which they call 'Blackfeet' in the States), Chippewa, Lakota, Assiniboine, and Métis, too. I can't even remember why I went but do remember liking how dry everything was. Even the forest was dry, inside the trees, the ground. Not like here, and really not like up where you're from. It was over near a town called Havre, which is a French word on account of the trappers who came down from Canada, from Hudson's Bay, but the Americans don't know nothing about French words so they say 'haver,' can you believe it? Stupid white people. Well, I guess they're not *so* stupid: they got our number pretty good, in'it? Yeah, it was south of Havre, on the Rocky Boy's Reservation, where the guy in your family went, Bad Bird, er Bad Bear."

Jim considered for a minute how or whether to respond. Carlton kept slapping his stomach while working his way almost to a reclined position on the couch. Laughter in the other room, dishes clanking in the kitchen. Jim tried not to look.

"I never heard any of that," Jim said. "I was away from my family from when I was about six."

"Yeah, I heard you was at Sturgeon Landing and then Guy Hill, huh? I was at Fort Alexander, and it was terrible. I can't believe those schools are still going. Luckily someone burned down Sturgeon Landing. A pissed off Native, no doubt. But then they just pushed you to Guy Hill, in'it? They pushed us too far, every day. Every day somebody new disappeared. No trace of 'em. Just gone. And if anyone said anything about it, asked a question like, 'Hey, what happened to so-and-so?', they'd get smacked, or worse. My sister got raped by a priest there. I was molested. For years. Catholics. Fuck."

"Yeah," Jim said. The thought of John tried to work its way into his head, but Jim fought it like he'd done since the time he ran away the first time and crept past the bare spot in the snow behind the boiler room.

"Did I hear you had a twin brother, too?" Carlton said.

"No."

❀ ❀ ❀ ❀ ❀ ❀

The next day Jim headed to Montana.

Reflections of Fall

Karen Colstrom

My Own Private Cold Mountain

Mark Walsh

I linger here off the marshes
South of a shrinking river

Watching a Cooper's hawk on power lines,
Red squirrels scramble up broken pines,

My neighbor walking his small dog.
On the trails behind my home

I hear air pushed
By cars on the highway,

Songs of robins in the Spring,
Call of barn owls in the deep night.

Some days I worry that I'm only
Good for making money. Other days

I forget that and keep alert for bald
eagles. We have them along the river

marsh - their numbers are growing,
And they don't care about your bank account.

Trumpeter Swan

Karen Colstrom

Statement to the Seward County Coroner

Steve Brisendine

Frank found her, all mud and snot
and tattered gingham, leaning back
against what was left of the windmill.

I remember a fencepost still standing,
pincushioned with straw, and a sheet
of tin wrapped around a splintered
cottonwood, and a tuft of some kind
of fur, soft yellow-brown, snagged on
some barbed wire.

The baby was past help by then, but
she wouldn't let it go.

She swore it was a little dog in a picnic
basket and sang to it, soft and slow;
I suppose it was a lullaby, but none
I ever heard before.

She wriggled ruined toes and called
them rubies; then her head drooped,
and we saw her bright blood.

She stopped singing, looked up at us,
murmured
Home...

then her feet beat together once, again,
again...and that was the end.

We found a blanket, closed her eyes,
covered her against the rain.

Silhouettes on a Country Road

Karen Colstrom

Continuum of Care

Deborah Ann Percy

Late Summer, First Chill

"I'm almost out of shaving cream," Albert says. He stands in the doorway of the hall leading into their living room, still holding the hand towel he used to wipe his freshly-shaved face. He is, of course, dressed for the day, now in khaki cargo pants and a blue Oxford-cloth shirt that could use an ironing but won't get it.

"Put it on the grocery list," Louise says. When her husband heads back down the hall instead and opens the front door to get the mail, she calls after him, "The list! On the kitchen counter. I've left a pen right with it." Knowing there will be no response—Albert has developed an aversion to her lists—she pushes up out of her chair, goes into their kitchen, and does it herself.

"There was only *The New Yorker*," he says when he reappears, magazine in one hand, damp towel still in the other.

"That was really all?"

"Just junk. I put it in the recycling basket on the porch."

"Sometimes I like to look at the junk," she says. Albert has tall kitchen wastebaskets for recycling in several supposedly-strategic places around their house, on the front porch below the mailbox. His definition of junk mail and hers is not always the same. "I put your shaving cream on the list," she says. "On the counter. In the kitchen."

"And we're out of biscuit-treats for Ruffy," he says, going off to read the magazine. He has a wooden kitchen chair on their small back porch where he likes to sit in the shade on hot summer afternoons.

Louise is stunned. "Are you trying to make me cry?" she says. Though she speaks softly, she knows he hears everything. But not this.

"My dear former colleague T.S. Bosco has an article in this issue," he says, half an hour later, letting the screened back-porch door slam behind him. He slaps the kitchen counter twice with the magazine. "He's forgotten once again that he's T. S. Bosco, not T. S. Eliot. He's also forgotten I actually knew George Harrison. *You* actually knew him. We were friends. We traded ukuleles."

She picks up the grocery list and pen from the floor where the violence of his envy over the success of his former university colleague has blown them off the counter. Now back outside, Albert flings the towel into their backyard where it lands on her one remaining rosebush.

"How are you feeling today?" he says when he comes back into the living room later, possibly as an apology—for the temper tantrum, for something else? He sits in his chair next to her, no *New Yorker* in sight. They have slightly mismatched overstuffed chairs with a table between them—all very well-used mission style. This is where they sit to read, to watch the news, sometimes to hold hands across the table that separates them. They call them their "Archie and Edith" chairs.

"I feel good," she says. "Better." But not really. There is something—maybe nothing?—an ache in her right side that has never been there before. Some foods that were her favorites she can no longer eat without throwing up. Their doctor had smiled at her benevolently and warned her as he would a child that if the simple diet changes he prescribed didn't work, he would certainly have to schedule some "more invasive tests."

"Princess Diana," Albert called her as they left the office.

"Having an affair with an old lover," she had responded, which shut him up for a minute or so. Albert is old, too. He sometimes forgets they started out together. She throws up; he forgets.

"T.S.'s article?" she says now, accepting his apology.

"Old bloviator," he says. "Some good lines in it, but I suspect Janet wrote them."

"I'm sorry. You deserve to be published everywhere," she says. "You and George were fast mates those last years."

"I did add to your shopping list," he says, probably a further apology. They are sliding back to normal. "The string you use to clean your teeth with?"

"Dental floss," she says.

"That's it," he says, happy that she understands him. "I deserve to be published everywhere instead of *The Sour Grapes Review* in Northern Michigan. Or the literary journal of Cherry Pit Junior College. What's for dinner? Should we go out?"

"Come on, Albert. You have an outstanding record of publications. And yes. Let's go out The new Belgian place?"

"Sounds good," he says. "I'll call and make a reservation. Can you have your pretty little self ready to go by six-thirty?" But he's not finished. Not yet ready to give up his grievance. *"Browning and His Teeny Tiny Circle of Friends."*

"Alberto, dear," she says gently.

"There you go with that Alberto business." He is really angry again, in a rage. "I hate Alberto."

"You hate my calling you Alberto? Since when?"

"It's demeaning. Belittling." He sits for a minute, gathers himself. "What shall we do about dinner? Shall I take you out?"

Louise wakes up suddenly in their dark bedroom. The moon shines through the apple tree and the open window, the leaves casting lacy shadows on the wall. A soft breeze smells of clove. He is not next to her, not in the room.

"Albert? Albert?"

She goes down the stairs, holding the banister to steady herself. In the dark kitchen, she sees through the screen door that Albert is sitting in his straight-backed chair on the porch.

"Dear Heart," she says, careful not to call him Alberto.

"I woke up and didn't know where I was. I didn't know who the old lady sleeping next to me was."

"Sweetheart." She sits on the top step and puts her hand still warm from the bed on his cold foot.

"George was my friend. You and Olivia would laugh and laugh. And yet…" He looks down at her. "It was you, wasn't it? In bed?" He touches her hair, silver in the moonlight. "It was, wasn't it? You who baked scones and laughed with Olivia?"

Fall, then Stupor

In late September, the old, untrimmed apple tree next to the back fence in the yard behind their home smells of applejack. The garden was a showplace when they bought the house forty years earlier. They entertained colleagues from the university out here, especially during the four years when Albert was department chair. College boys, and eventually girls, too, had raked dead

leaves out of the flower beds in the spring. They cut back the daffodils when warm weather withered them, mowed and watered the grass—thick in the center and sparse under the big tree— took away the trimmings from Louise's roses, and collected rotting apples off the ground in the fall. Now she and Albert pretty much enjoy the yard wild. The fermenting apples now litter the base of the untrimmed fruit tree that has grown as tall as their own roof. Bees grow drunk feasting on the rotting fruit.

Because they had dogs over the years, the yard was fenced in with cedar that weathered gray and eventually wore out. When a section fell in during a Michigan spring storm, their last dog Ruffy, a small smart beagle, took months to realize it was gone and that he was free to roam. He gave up his bachelor life, disappearing for days. Ruffy's disappearances made Albert anxious. He'd wander around the neighborhood whistling for the dog. Ruffy always came back eventually for Louise's kibble and table scraps. He had died in the spring. Their last dog.

Now they sit on the leaf-covered flagstone patio in their Adirondack chairs, newly repainted a pleasing bright yellow They salute each other with their first of two daily Manhattans always made with their favorite bourbon—Maker's Mark.

"I saw a gadget on Facebook designed to help old farts get up out of chairs like this," Louise says, slapping the shiny arm of her chair.

"Shovel, is it?" Albert says, taking a sip of his drink. "Forklift?"

"A blue plastic thing with handles on both ends that one person uses to pull the other up," she says. "Of course, someone has to be already off their butt and on their feel to make it work."

"Or remember where somebody left it lying around," he says.

"That, too."

"Mother? Daddy?" a voice with just a touch of hysterical drama rings from inside the house.

"She's arrived," Louise says and calls," We're out in back, dear!"

"Did we know she was coming?" Albert says.

"We did." Louise holds up a finger. "Let me do the talking."

"Here you are." Their daughter Eleanor bursts through the screen door and lets it bang behind her. She's very thin—possibly anorexic?—and taller than either of her parents. Today she is dressed as always in a suit, accessorized with a lot of jewelry she inherited from her grandmother, Louise's mother. "What a mess this yard is. What's happened to the boys you hire to keep this place looking respectable?"

"Grew up," Louise says.

"Went to college, got married, had a daughter," Albert says, then sits back in his chair when he sees Louise's warning look. He has mellowed over the last few months. Less angry, he is sliding into quiet, forgetful compliance.

"You're not ready," Eleanor says. "Don't tell me you forgot, too, Mother."

"Your mother?" Albert says. "Forget?"

"Of course we didn't," Louise says, lifting a reminding finger in his direction.

"You can't go dressed like that," Eleanor says. "And you're drinking."

"We do plan to drink Manhattans there," Louise says. "This isn't a Methodist place we're looking at, is it?"

"And recycle," Albert says, joining in.

"Please, Mother. Daddy. Freshen up a bit. Are those pajama pants you're wearing?"

"Flannel, dear," Louise says, extending a brightly patterned leg. "I believe they expect us at three."

"Strain the ice. Manhattans in the fridge." Albert says, rocking his butt back and forth toward the edge of his Adirondack until he can get up. Then he holds out his hand to help Louise.

"Dear God," Eleanor says, "what have you done to your chairs? Daddy, did you pick out that hideous color?

"I thought this guy..." Louise says, unfastening her seat belt.

"Tom Kent. The Director of Admissions," Eleanor says. She has pulled her Volvo into a parking lot outside a six-story building that looks like a dorm from the seventies.

"Right," Louise says, holding back any smart-ass comments on the title. "I thought Mr. Kent was showing us their signature semi-detached homes at the beginning of their continuum of care."

"He's meeting us here," Eleanor says. "You'll have to pass a few tests to qualify for an individual home."

"Tests," Albert says with a hint of the old rage in his voice.

"To see if you're still capable of living on your own," Eleanor says, trying to be reassuring.

"Living on our own!" Albert says, voice rising. An elderly woman hirpling forward pauses to turn and look at him.

"Albert, dear," Louise warns, taking his arm. "They will check our blood pressure."

"You mean like 'Person. Woman. Man. Camera, TV'?" He glares at Eleanor. "That test?"

Louise takes a firm grip on his arm, and they follow Eleanor who has gone ahead. They are ushered into the director's office by a twelve-year-old boy dressed as an adult in shirt and tie. Tom Kent, whom Louise thinks looks disturbingly like Tom Hiddleston, holds out his hand to Albert, who only takes it after a nudge from her.

"Welcome to Colony Village," he says, his distinct Michigan accent, confirming immediately that he is not the English actor. "Eleanor thought we could start here before looking at more independent options."

"Did she," Albert says.

"Did you, Dear," Louise says.

"There are several levels of care in this specific module," Tom Kent says. "Also exercise facilities. Music rooms with updated piano tuning, and a dining room with a two-star chef."

"All for the same $400,000 buy-in price as the independent home?" Louise says. "Plus the additional $3,500 a month?"

"We provide a continuum of care," Kent says.

"And would we be assured we could stay together?" Louise says.

"What?" Albert says.

"We do the best we can," Kent says.

"Mother," Eleanor says to Louise, as if she is being rude.

"And what happens if we run out of money?"

"Mother, please." And then to Kent, "They're not going to run out of money, I can assure you."

"And we drink the...New York drink," Albert says.

"Manhattans," Louise says. "Two at the end of each day."

"Of course, you may drink alcohol if you choose," Kent says with a smile. "As long as it's not contraindicated by your medications."

An hour later back at Eleanor's car, Louise secures a frowning Albert's backseat seatbelt. He is humming "My Sweet Lord." She stands and closes the door to find her daughter still beside her. "Oh, Mother," Eleanor says, gripping her inherited amethyst necklace. "I'm sure everyone here will love Daddy."

"What a horror," Albert says when they are back in their kitchen, their daughter safely on her way to her office. "I thought we were looking at a home. In a house. Not a grim two-room apartment with an elevated toilet seat in the bathroom."

"We have a plan, dear," Louise says. "We're not going anywhere. Especially if you leave the talking to me." She hands him his re-iced Manhattan.

"I've talked all my life. I made my living talking to students."

"I would have suggested against saying you'd rather plunge off the bridge of San Luis Rey than live there."

"This Clark Kent fellow. He looks like someone we know." Albert takes a big gulp of his drink and sinks down in a kitchen chair.

"Tom Hiddleston, the actor. *Henry V.* Shakespeare." She sits on the chair across from him. "Plantagenet. Band of Brothers. Married a French girl. Died young."

"Oh, yes. But the voice was off." He takes another gulp, draining his glass. "Whiny and Midwestern. And everything he said was awful."

"That our continuums of care may take different paths. But we would still be free to visit each other."

"No," Albert says. "I won't stop sleeping with that strange old woman in my bed."

"No," she says, pleased at his joke at the end of their harrowing day.

"How about another...of our New York City drinks?

"Manhattans? It's still warm enough to have our second drink out in the back yard."

Deep Winter, Letting Go

They have a plan. Actually, it's a continuum of options. They've joked about it for years, but after their visit to Colony Village, it's no longer humorous. They don't speak about a plan at all.

Then a Michigan thaw occurs in mid-January. Temperatures hover just under sixty degrees for almost a week, and for a time no icy wind is blowing in off the big lake. The sun is a weak sister during the days. Late one afternoon, Louise puts on sweatpants and the pretty pink sweater with "easy" big buttons Eleanor gave her for Christmas. She goes outside to wipe the debris off their Adirondack chairs, which glow in fading sun. She and Albert—who is wrapped in a thick scarf and zippered into his heavy winter parka because he is always cold—sit in the darkening glow, drinking their New-York-City drinks. They point out to each other small patches of daffodil spears poking like daggers through the rotting leaves in their flower beds. They both wear the white orthopedic tennis shoes Eleanor has bullied them into buying.

"The...spring flowers have been fooled," Albert says.

"Daffodils," she prompts. "It's happened to them before. They're flexible."

They sit in silence for a long time, sipping their drinks. The next round is in a shaker on the ground between them—Louise's suggestion to save one of them a trip back into the house. A full super moon rises and stays close to the horizon, surrounded by what seems like a halo of ice crystals.

Albert clears his throat. "I think we need an idea...a road-guide...of what to do. Next. Now."

"We do," Louise says.

"I vote for refusing to go anywhere," Albert says, his voice growing stronger like the early spring flowers.

"That should be an option," Louise says. "I've Googled 'Old farts staying in their own homes.' Aging in place they call it."

"The woman who was here the other day," he says, pleased he understands. "The one with the fuzzy red..." He pats the top of the old cloth cap on his head.

"Hair," she assists.

"Ugly white plastic bars," he says, his voice growing stronger.

"White so aged eyes can find them. They'll get us up and down stairs a while longer." And after another pause, "There are other options." There is one she's been considering for months. Eleanor is leaving in a day for a conference in D.C. And the day after that the temperatures will plunge to near zero. Another trick of Michigan weather. "When it's cold again, really cold, we come out here and spend the night. Frozen solid in the morning. Old couple dies tragically. Full of booze. Holding hands."

"Sounds like *Ethan Frome*," Albert says, his voice clearer than it has been in months. "And you know how that worked out."

"I do. I've considered that possibility." They sit, his mittened hand on her bare one.

"And what if it's Eleanor who finds us?"

"That would be hard for her."

"I've been considering possibilities, too. I think I prefer a blaze of glory," Albert says, his voice still strong. "Eleanor's six-shooters are still in the basement somewhere. You call the police. Say a crazy old man is threatening you. We come down the front porch steps, cap guns blazing. Like Butch and...Sunshine." She forbears correcting him, and he continues. "We're not going to Community Horror Home for the Aged."

"No, we're not," she says. "I'm afraid we've moved closer to the end of their continuum of care. Manhattans would definitely be contra-indicated. They might mix with our meds and kill us."

"We could move into Eleanor's guest room," he says. They both laugh and then smile.

"Shall we vote?" she says.

"Shall we just stay?" he says.

"I think so," she says. "I definitely think we should give it a try."

"Did we walk Ruffy?" he says.

"IIe's good," she says, and realizes he has fallen asleep. "Dear Alberto" she says, her hand warm under his mitten.

A shift in the rising moon catches another patch of sharp daffodil knives, silver in the light. Louise sees that the foolish flowers have continued to grow as she and Albert continue to sit in their chairs.

Hunger Song

Steve Brisendine

My right wiper blade
chirps on the inswing;

the car seems beset
by a persistent sparrow,

begging for bits of the
bread riding shotgun.

It sounds too much like
a bedraggled real thing

to the part of me that
dreads rooflessness

on nights when nothing
shows signs of abating.

Painting 3095

Claudio Parentela

Blue

Devon Neal

Finally at the front of the line
of the snowcone truck, parked downtown
near the fountain's measured chaos,
we watch as the vendor shaves
thin slivers of delicate ice, each one
like a soft clear coin, molding them
together into a porous mound
like a shimmering brain. I ask my son
what flavor he wants, and he responds,
"blue." It's a tinkling trickle
from the dolphin-nosed bottle pourer
and his snowcone is stained a deep azure,
and as we walk side by side in the afternoon sun,
I think of swirling salt crystals in the sea,
the sharp polar edges of arctic ice,
the needle-fuzzed curve of a mountain's spine,
the hot sizzle of lightning bone,
or if today, in one of these rare moments
that we spend together, just us,
he knows what the sky tastes like.

Within the Wilds

Jennifer Weigel

Terminal Rondo

E.H. Jacobs

If I stopped believing in time,
     I might meet your sarcasm without anger.

If I stopped believing in anger,
     I would place my arm around your sorrows,

If I could stop aching with sorrow,
     laughter could suspend my gravity.

But, if I untethered from this gravity,
     I fear being consumed by longing.

If I escaped the binds of longing,
     the void would fill with expectations.

If I could obliterate expectations,
     I'd pray your illness would not progress.

And I would want to halt that progress,
     but your illness would take no mind.

So I drown out my clattering mind,
     and your body degrades and wastes.

When I turn my eye from your wasting,
     I trip on the crag of necessity.

Then I refuse to trust in necessity,
     and I am crushed by the vagaries of choice.

I deny the imperatives of choice,
     and instead I anchor in me.

When faith falters in the soundness of me,
     I question the value of life.

As I become unmoored in life,
     I seek hope in reconciliation.

But I cannot heal in reconciliation,
     as you soon will run out of time.

Theories of Resurrection

Richard Marranca

Now, after the expired friendship of long ago, the Victorian house seemed smaller and encroached by nature. Michelle Goodyear felt like a child overwhelmed by mystery.

The teacher, Gabriel Macaulay, had been a truth bringer, a visionary. Michelle pondered what he had been and why the group became seekers and seemed to need him more than anything.

"I only wondered when, not if, you'd come," Anna Macaulay, said, offering her hand like something melting.

From the porch, Anna and Michelle drifted into the living room, which had lots of faded brass and Asian carpets. A book on gardening lay on the coffee table. Anna had widened and smelled of herbs. So many years had passed that, paradoxically, the years erased themselves, and time seemed young again, as it is in The Bhagavad Gita. Anna's charm and elegance had not diminished in any sense.

"I'll get my cane. Then shall we walk along the hedgerow?"

With a turn of the skeleton key, they exited the side door and sank in the moist grass.

"Purple flowers," said Michelle, inhaling the fragrances as if one could distill the past.

Anna smiled with tight lips. "He's very sick."

Michelle gave a slight bow. "Sorry. I heard about--."

"You're the first of the group to return."

Michelle nodded. Anna poked at clay pots with her shoe.

"He had a more heroic view of the end than this."

"Yes, he would," Michelle replied.

"Ah, you were the one with wit," Anna said, perking up. "We're ready to go at our age; the fulfillment of life and all that. Finished -- the job nearly done. He gave so much, had so much. I'm afraid when you all left him, he left himself. No, don't say anything. Inevitable, wasn't it? The greatest students are rebels, right? The nature of brilliance. We both knew that. He accepted it, that torture."

"Perhaps," Michelle began to say.

"A teacher is a mirror of what's best inside us. But one shouldn't get stuck there with the teacher. He was a confused man, but not a confused teacher."

Michelle looked toward the treetops. "Yes."

Michelle rubbed her eyes, while the wife gave a bewildered grin in anticipation of something that remained unsaid. They walked silently along the roses and a statue of Demeter, which one of his students had brought from Crete. The breeze cooled the midday swelter that stifled any urgency.

Her apron full of gardening tools sticking out like weaponry, Anna stepped carefully. She had a lovely flow of silver hair with curls at the ends. Michelle remembered when Anna seemed jealous of all the young people coming to the house: experimenters and seekers, druggies and dropouts, students and family types -- mountain climbers of the soul.

For Gabriel and Anna, it must have felt like the first steps into the underworld when the house turned quiet.

Michelle thought Anna must have had a difficult life with him, and that even now with his sickness, there'd be none of the students around to transform her into The Great One, The Mother, the one connected to the source of mystery and abundant life. Really the one who stuck with Gabriel. Anna would not get that kind of payback or refund. How much had Anna understood him then? She must have found his aggrandizement and followers to be overwhelming. In the old days, Anna made tea and took care of everything, holding the group together without anyone being aware of it.

"Fig trees," said Michelle, seeing the broad silvery green leaves and knobs ready to turn into fruit. "Who does all this work? It's marvelous."

"I do. In late fall, I cover the fig trees so it's not cold for them. He loves figs. He identifies too much with that other fig-eater, Socrates," Anna said with a giggle. "Or was it Odysseus?"

"Or Fig Newton."

They laughed and grabbed at each other's hands. A magnolia tree shielded them from the fermenting sun, and a dusty chair beside it seemed forgotten. There was a swing nearby and a thick row of hedges obscuring a gate. Some gargoyles, frogs and saints spied from the greenery. Michelle and Gabriel had spent long hours in discussion here.

Gabriel never traveled much.

As they returned to the house, Michelle remembered when Gabriel and Anna argued while she cooked and how afterward, he said "the food contained anger." Gabriel would put his hand over the table to remove the negative energy. Sometimes Gabriel was stoic, sometimes unexplainable, loving but distant.

Even now, Michelle believed him to be the most erudite person one could meet. He taught by inspiration and sheer weighty knowledge and the experience of one who meditated hours each day and read even more. He was charismatic, wise, an unknown world figure. He had been a world-class athlete too – he had that physicality and confidence that others knew from imagination only.

"Perhaps you want to see him now," said Anna.

"Oh. Sure."

Gabriel was wrapped up in sheets, mummy-like, and his once proud frame was decimated. Everything was smaller except for his proud hawk nose. One foot ended in a bandaged square and the blonde lion's mane of hair was reduced to wiry strands. Yet he still possessed a handsome mountain glow, a touch of the long-legged highlander that once raised a sword to smite falsity. Michelle turned toward the door, but Anna was behind her, eager and sentinel-like in her blue dress.

"He's not in pain, is he?" Michelle asked.

"Beyond pain. The pain was before," the wife said with a hitchhiking gesture.

Michelle patted Gabriel on the head but, realizing the almost sacrilegious nature of her act, touched his shoulder. As the sun penetrated the windows in geometric swaths of light and dark, some branches whisked against the panes.

"Is it, my dear, my most dear -- Michelle Goodyear?" his voice cracked as he propped himself up, then he nodded in recognition. "Here at last."

"I am. It's okay to visit?" Michelle asked.

"Always," Gabriel and Anna said in unison. "Always and forever."

Anna held Michelle's hand. Then she pulled the chain of the brass lamp on the table and checked to see if Gabriel had eaten. The oatmeal was cement, but he had sipped the herbal juice.

The rosette design on the wallpaper seemed like a wall of time, of witnessing, just like the Horus eyes on ancient Egyptian coffins.

"Michelle, you're here," he rejoiced in a wavering voice. "How are you?"

"I'm fine. But you, my old friend. How are you feeling?"

"Not the best, but if you fight it, you lose. Once you gain a little light, you see the drama and entertainment that is life and society. Same with your own life."

She smiled, catching a glimpse of old slippers on the floor.

She wondered how time had passed for him now. He had so many interests, such glimmering abilities and imagination, that she knew he would prefer to learn something even in his last breath. Alongside one wall sat immense bookshelves separated by paintings and a figure in lotus position with the seven chakras bursting from the body. She noticed his university degrees on the wall. He never mentioned that. She had thought he was a rich kid and an autodidact—he was neither. He was one of those people who learn what matters after formal education. He was panoramic and rounded in the way that people could not be anymore, the modern tragedy.

"A burst of light, you are."

"I meant to come for a while," she said, her face expansive and glowing, portraying all the emotions.

"You're here now."

"There are many people we haven't seen in ages," added Anna.

"The others often mention you," said Michelle. "I spoke to Bobby Rossi during the holidays. He owns a few stores, even an old book and record shop. He still teaches yoga. Kathy is a chiropractor. Smith is a CEO."

"Anna, did you hear that?"

"What, oh yes," she replied. "Just working on a list of our twenty favorite films."

"That's Anna's strategy for keeping me alive. She knows lists bedevil me. I've made lists since childhood."

"Like Ben Franklin," Anna replied.

"We lost some time, Michelle, that's all," he offered. "What's time? People still can't explain it better than Kant or Augustine."

Michelle nodded, sat down. "Yeah," she said, looking down at her trembling knees, then at the Tibetan rug with the lion in the center.

"Who knows where we'd all be by now?" Gabriel said.

"Those years were special, never-to-be-repeated."

"Gabriel, don't tire yourself out. Have you a need for the oatmeal heated?" asked Anna. "Let's have tea and scones for Michelle."

"Oh swell," he said, with a cough and a smile.

Anna grabbed her cane and headed to the kitchen. The hum of the attic fan drowned out his weighty breaths. Michelle looked around at the elegant retreat this English woman created so Gabriel could dabble in terrestrial & cosmic questions, which Anna once pronounced "as important as the number of angels on a pin."

In the early days, Michelle thought him a henpecked husband -- and Anna morganatic, jealous, meddling. Michelle soon came to realize – and realized it now more than ever – that she'd been terribly mistaken about Anna: that the husband knew things, but that the wife lived them.

"What can I get for you?" asked Michelle.

He cleared his throat, twisting his torso in order to breathe.

"I'm okay, really. Getting old cuts out that annoying chatter in the head. Just wonderful. But I'd like an extra ten years – that's how long it took Odysseus to reach home. I was working on something. I never wrote anything during those years. The spoken word has the music and honesty of birdsong and wolf howling. Writing's too blunt and fixed. Dear, do you teach?"

Anna returned with a tray of tea and scones, along with Bettys Milk Chocolate Guineas and Fruit Jellies. She held up her hands, patting the air, encouraging them to continue as she exited the living room. She had started with energy but now almost crawled away in exhaustion.

"Lovely, thanks so much, Anna," said Michelle, then turning to Gabriel. "I did but not recently. Things changed."

"Remember that trip I sent you on to Sedona. March 19 –" he suddenly screeched.

Michelle put her fingers on her chin. "Quite a memory, quite a trip."

"The things I had in mind for all of you. Sorry." Gabriel rubbed his forehead, then adjusted his hearing aid. He flicked at some tears.

Michelle closed her eyes for a moment. She walked around the room. She ran her hand across some antique books on the top shelf. The room was still except for dust sparkling like snowflakes.

"Michelle, what do you do?"

"I'm head of counseling at the college. I like it."

"Admirable. Those young ones keep you on your toes. I can only imagine how much you help them."

Michelle nodded sideways. "First time I met you, you gave a talk on genius – geniuses look at problems from all angles and see what others miss. Geniuses make their own luck! You said to read biographies for inspiration; the great lives would make us better. Start with Plutarch. College was never so inspiring."

Gabriel suddenly got energized like a dragon that had been slumbering. Anna made some noise in the kitchen.

"Those are my favorites on the shelf over there," Gabriel pointed. "You see, the world is a cult. Of science, of materialism, of religion, politics, even art. Humans can't cool down their horrid instincts. I gave you the tools to see it. We were like renegade monks at the end of the day debating. But you taught me about compassion, about the care of nature, too. You young ones annoyed and modernized me."

"I hope I get that back," she said, her hands open.

"You never lose what you are. Go down into your treasure," he said. "If you knew how I felt about you and the others."

"You never showed it. Just criticism."

"That. I was too eager. 'Narrow is the path like a razor's edge,'" Gabriel said. Then he stretched his arms and laughed. "The ancients knew how the gods play jokes on us. Forgive me if I was dumb."

"Hey old man, did you ever figure out that dilemma from the *Bhagavad Gita* about Arjuna seeing the opposing army?" Michelle asked.

She pushed her chair closer to him.

"Back then, I would've emphasized duty more. I would've been yang-oriented and said he should fight and kick his cousins' butts and not worry about the fruits of victory and whether he'd die or kill others. Now I'd say Arjuna should not fight in the war. He should get on his chariot and fuck the gods and his duty and flee to where there's peace. Maybe a cave, maybe find some girlfriends, like those lovely Gopis. Duty, such humbug."

Michelle laughed. "Whatever."

"We have so much to discuss. Where did Anna go? I love her, but she won't let me curse."

"You could curse," Michelle replied, pointing her finger at him.

"Always been a failing. Why I never took up the teaching trade and kept to humble jobs."

"I curse now too."

"There's much to curse in this world. But yes, don't curse in front of the old Englishwoman," Gabriel replied in a thin voice. "I know you can't stay much longer. When will you be back?"

"I'll be back. Soon. I'll bring you something I've been writing, a memoir sort of and I've added lots about you. I mainly want to capture that experience and time."

He gasped softly. "My oars are vanishing in the water, little time left for anything," he replied. "I wish I could help. But I've lost some of the light, the clarity."

"No, it's waiting," Michelle said, and kissed his cheek.

After a few minutes of small talk and goodbyes, Anna walked Michelle to the door and embraced her.

On the way home, Michelle imagined Gabriel's encounter in the 1950s with a yogi from South India, a Brahman named Vishnu, simply referred to as "the Teacher." With Gatsby-like charm, Gabriel, on an afternoon off from his executive job on Wall Street, had met this guru by accident in the Egyptian gallery of the Metropolitan Museum of Art. Gabriel stood there at the beginning of East meets West, or so it seemed.

The guru, contemplating the serene statues, smiled at Gabriel, then asked, "Do you know the Egyptians viewed the afterlife in multiple ways?"

"One seems enough," replied Gabriel. "But what is death?"

"Death? Perhaps your best ally to achieve the good life."

They had tea and became friends. Gabriel could explain the modern world to the guru who initiated him into yoga and meditation, which were like a big secret then. Michelle did not know how much of this story was true, but it seemed appropriate based on her observation that major events in one's life cannot be foreseen and happen quietly: like love, like death. She had seen the guru's picture, a dark man in a brushstroke of white clothes, using a cane.

She drove past farmhouses and horses, surrounded by fences set like long teeth. Amidst the cradle of hills, trees poked out in a great blend and a lake emerged. She parked her car. The birds eased her mind back to the child-depths of past decades, back to running along the breaking waves, fearful of a lone boat floating on the lake's respiration, a boat tempted away by the current, but arrested by a rope. This was the central image of life, the diametric nature of everything, its impossible balance.

She stretched out on the scratchy pillow of pine needles. Her mind wandered from the emerald moss and trees, from thought to thought, fear to fear. She hoped that her visit was a way to make peace with Gabriel and Anna.

Michelle wanted to help him realize what he had done for others, as well as salvage her own life from the middle-aged complacency and acceptance of the unacceptable. After the great bloodlettings in the 1960s, when she first met Gabriel, she was wild and believed in all the rebellions of the time; it was not that she disbelieved in them now, but that life went on no matter what -- the flashes of her being could not ameliorate the sea of melancholy and pain. She lost the clarity and urgency out of which the rebellions sprang. Age had taught her that darkness accompanies light.

Michelle felt buffeted by guilt but realized that fate is a cruel parent and that one makes peace, or not. She parked in the driveway between the two birdhouses that were miniature replicas of her house.

She went to her back porch and sat on the wicker chair.

Her mind drifted into a meditation that he taught them, "The Throne Room." She went down a few steps, really feeling them in her knees, into the darkness, where the water dripped unseen. Alone. In the throne room she could have anything. It frightened her at first, but her senses calmed. Michelle could hear his voice guiding her though corridors and secret places; just as quickly the voice faded.

Michelle saw her childhood cat and bicycle. She found herself in the empty burial chamber in The Great Pyramid, where she had been three decades ago in the company of a man who was lost to her somewhere in Boston, as good as dead, lost like the pharaohs. She found a pile of jewels and kicked it aside, laughing inwardly; she was not a tomb robber. She felt released from the hard mechanism of consciousness.

That evening, she had dinner. She read passages from a book by Vivekananda. She retired early to her bedroom. She called her old friend, Bobby, but the number was out of order. She could not accommodate her own enthusiasm, but for what?

Even half asleep, she wondered where time had fled. Time, the way one experienced it, was a blend of past, present, future. She thought constantly about Gabriel, as if such remembering could keep the snakes in her life underground. She feared that, after all these years, there might not be a chance to see him again. She suddenly wanted to know what she had learned and who she was...

What Gabriel had taught was too vast to explain – not the usual categorized knowledge from books, but something beyond that, the ability to create and be there at the beginning. To find stillness in chaos. To remake the self, to think you could remake society. To know that your goals were essential for humanity's evolution. He trained their minds to be raw and free, or rather he untrained their minds. He gave them the experiences of an original mind; he had them read the great books of the world, to read for self-realization, not to throw ideas around like marbles. The intellect was never a game for Gabriel, never an academic wine & cheese party. He insisted. "You don't do that, so why say it?" was his favorite line. He spoke about history, myth, archaeology, anthropology, art, philosophy, physics, music, science, business, economics, money, about being comprehensive. "Spirit and ideas are the garden from which everything grows," he had said.

At times, Gabriel and Anna played the role of salon leaders, but Gabriel could do this with a twist -- yoga postures and meditation. A spiritual salon, a new Athens, a new America. Anything seemed possible back then.

Gabriel molded them into a group with intricate and generous finances – their money. He purchased a building and gave up his job as a Wall Street executive to be their teacher. He had the group scour the world like children searching for Easter Eggs: to a village near Chichicastenango to meet a shaman; Auroville to learn about kundalini and utopia; Stonehenge and Taos to learn about sacred landscape; Delphi, Cusco and Rome to learn about the axis mundi; Walden and Monticello to understand idealism; New Orleans to learn about music...

Upon returning, the travelers shared their experiences.

Michelle awoke with the sunlight, moist with sleeping tears, before the chimes of her clock. She rushed into her car, heading for Gabriel's house. She felt possessed. Moved by guilt, fear, love.

She raced along the shadowy road that soon erupted with the colors of Monarch Butterflies. She pondered Gabriel's ability to inspire others and played an old tape: he took a statement from the Buddha – "'Don't waste a minute of your life in your quest for enlightenment'"– and infuse it with such blood that you actually thought it best not to waste a moment, that you could use all your time, even when eating or walking, for some addition to your treasure. (Gabriel created the labyrinth and then exposed the riddles, the truth and the way out, but it seemed like your truth before you knew it.)

Michelle saw the hedges first. She parked her car, careful not to slam the door. It was odd that someone seemed to be sitting in the garden. Through the morning mist, Michelle followed the path that reached the garden.

She moved closer. Not looking down, Michelle tripped over a statue. It broke.

"Anna, are you okay?" asked Michelle. "What is it?"

But it was Gabriel with a cane by his feet. She saw him through the greenery and, for a moment, thought she might be fantasizing. But he was there, a man who could still surprise you, who destroyed insignificance with anti-moments bursting with meaning, with meaning turned into a last gasp.

Michelle hurried toward him, grimly asking, "Gabriel, you're alone?"

He struggled to speak. "It frees the mind. When the body's stiff, the mind soon follows."

He attempted to stand on his head, almost did it.

Michelle ran to the front door, and looked in. Pounded the door. A poster of the Beatles, with mop heads and Nehru collars, seemed to speak or sing.

Bare silence for endless minutes. Finally, Anna came down in her nightgown.

Anna and Michelle carried Gabriel back to his bed, sometimes dragging him. He mumbled all the way – though there were flashes of consciousness -- and could not hold up his body.

"Even after fifty years together, I wonder if I understand him," Anna said, looking around amidst the quietude.

"Mystery isn't a bad thing," replied Michelle.

Anna suddenly lifted her head.

The Coneflowers Are Falling

Suzanna C. de Baca

The coneflowers are beginning to lean.
The bright magenta of the bloom is fading
ever so slightly on one petal, edges
browning like burnt paper on another.
I panic, counting on my hands again
and again: *March, April, May, June, July.*
Six to twelve months the doctor told you,
but I have been down this road before,
so my mind sticks on *six, six, six,*
a ticking clock, a deadline.

The Russian sage is beginning to droop,
falling on its side, pungent and heavy,
lavender tubes threatening to collapse.
The bell-shaped hosta buds, pale periwinkle
and cream, balancing on slender stalks,
begin to shrink and wither, just slightly,
imperceptibly at first, but the signs are clear:
summer is ending. I read the date on paper,
but deny it in my heart, ripping the calendar
pages, crumbling them like brittle leaves,
burying them deep in the trash can.

I refuse to let the coneflowers fall.
Look at me: I'll hold the stems back
with my bare hands, stand in front
of them, arms outstretched, protecting
them from the passage of time,
bargaining for just one more month.

"It's time to tie up the phlox," my grandmother
said shortly before she died. She knew
she could not will the flowers to stay,
only steady them, only breathe them in
a little longer. But I am not ready.

Deep Inside the Sun

Suzanna C. de Baca

I do not believe in angels,
but I do believe in clouds.
I do not believe in heaven,
but I do believe in the sun.
You appeared there, suddenly,
in the rays streaming down
on the bay at the end of day,
your brilliant, sparkling beams
penetrating the sea, golden
arms reaching from the nimbus,
ivory aura glowing so clearly
against the shadowed backdrop
of the mountains, dancing
on the surface of the water,
a dervish whirling wildly,
your presence so vivid,
your voice as plain as day
in the din of the dining room,
over the hum of conversation,
crystal clinking, silver clanking,
as if you were sending up
a flare, pointing, *"Over here!"*
I was overcome, all at once faint,
short of breath. But I rose,
alone, trembling, and walked
to the bar, steadied myself
against a stone column
on the corner of the balcony,
and stood, looking at you,
radiant light, still here,
still shimmering in the sky,
still blazing against the bay,
still shining, luminous,
deep inside the sun.

Special Section
of
Poetry and Art

Reflecting Each Other

Vessels

Lynn Pattison

plaster cloth and natural elements

Vessels

Lynn Pattison

Gall

wasp eggs on an oak tree.
Woody orb swells from branch,
encases and protects—a golden nursery,
hard-shelled. A single larva inside, yellow-green
symmetry: thin membranes radiating from the center, holy
monstrance for a small god.   **Hive**   Papery hub. Hum
of community. Eggs laid and hatched, the business of reproduce
and nurture a steady thrum. Meanwhile sunlight's turned to golden
honey, hints of rosemary, clover. Hives in the ground are a grim surprise
to children at play. Hives in the wall warm the room. I've not seen them
in cemeteries but hear they exist. Haunted honey   **Nest**   Open-air
casita. Cup-sized or immense on stony outcrop or tucked in chimney ivy.
Sewn. Woven. Mud-daubed and lined with breast feathers. Life hatches,
grows, fledges from the bowl-built nursery. There are nests on the floor
of the forest and in sand by tufts of seagrass. Oriole sacs hang among
big-leaved squash vines.   **Pouch**   The wild's mobile home, where a
just-viable joey climbs to its snug apartment to feed and grow. Never
worried about getting lost. Granted, it gets cramped eventually, but as
every New Yorker understands—it's what's available.   **Ovary**   Life's
vestibule—eggs in the bank, vibrating with probability. Fecund glow
like a halo. In garden, forest, house and cavern, in the deepest lake,
ovaries, pregnant with life. Cross-section beautiful as any oak gall.
My heart turns when I remember that girls grow tiny ovaries,
a life's worth of shiny, pearling eggs, before they are born.
Egg   Universe in a room. Nucleus of eternity, fertility.
Gigantic to miniscule, with just-right hard walls.
If you want to see a god, this is where
you look. Children know egg
geometry early. See the forms
they make from mud or clay?

Mask in Tree

Margaret Laird Dornin

Rooms

Christopher L. Dornin

My mother died in her sleep
Her body, bed and oxygen
had moved to new rooms
by nine. We sat on her floor
among the mysteries she fondled
and the webs she couldn't sweep.

By afternoon she was dust.
I watched her paint with a knife
a gull on the ground with folded
wings. It broods beside a fallen
nest with three eggs.
I'm one of those eggs.

A yellow mask watches
the imperiled bird from a tree
more motion than mortal wood.
A gold cloud floats
from the mask like a second head.
A blue glow from these

and these rooms beyond the frame
illuminates the falling snow.
My wife's long hair
emerges from that painting
in my videos of her playing piano
solos for the church website

in this Covid winter of distance
worship. Parkinson's slows
her left hand. She repeats
musical phrases until her fingers
trill like hummingbird wings
beneath her moving face and arms.

Head in Shell

Margaret Laird Dornin

Conch

Christopher L. Dornin

My mother painted this Rorschach
smear of a massive shell,
thick with successful accidents.

She laid them on with a trowel.
A slab across the top of the work
bends into an oxen yoke,

then morphs into the prong of an anchor
stabbing the shell. The conch
gleams like a photograph, but it's rich

with visual puns. The shell
bleeds into a slice of the living
diaphragm, then forms a hood

that drapes around a bearded head
with gaping holes for eyes.
Her blind monk drifts

in the blue depths of the sea,
then grows into a constellation.
He can wait for ages to breathe.

Contributors' Notes

Christine Andersen is a retired dyslexia specialist who hikes daily in the Connecticut woods, pen and pad in pocket, hounds at her heels. Many of her poems are inspired by the outdoors. Publications include *The Comstock Review, The Octillo Review, Awakenings Review, Gyroscope Review, Evening Street Review, SLAB, The Dewdrop, Glimpse, DASH, Rushing through the Dark,* and *Glassworks,* among others. She won the 2023 *American Writers Review* Poetry Contest.

Brian C. Billings is a professor of English and drama at Texas A&M University-Texarkana, where he also serves as the editor-in-chief for *Aquila Review.* His poems have appeared in *Abandoned Mine, Ancient Paths, Argestes, The Bluebird Word, Confrontation, Evening Street Review, Glacial Hills Review,* and *The Woven Tale Press.* Publishers for his scripts include Eldridge Publishing and Heuer Publishing.

Steve Brisendine lives, works and remains unbeaten against the New York Times crosswords in Mission, KS. A 2024 Pushcart Prize nominee, he has appeared in two *Best of Choeofpleirn Press* collections, as well as in *Modern Haiku, Flint Hills Review, I-70 Review,* and other publications and anthologies.

Kyler Campbell is an Assistant Professor of Writing at Charleston Southern University. His creative work has appeared in the *Cumberland River Review, Flash Fiction Magazine, Sheepshead Review, Driftwood Press,* and elsewhere. He lives in Charleston, South Carolina with his wife, two girls, and their 80-pound lapdog named Bear.

Clarissa Cervantes is a travel researcher photographer. Clarissa also supplies freelance articles on a variety of topics for newspaper, blogs, websites, and magazines such as USA Today. Clarissa's photo gallery includes images from all over the world, where she finds inspiration to share her photographs with others through her creative lens, inviting the viewer to question the present, look closer, explore more the array of emotions, and follow the sunlight towards a brighter future.

Karen Colstrom is a native born Kansan who grew up on the farm. She has a background in art, graduating from Emporia State University. Karen taught a children's program for 20 years, sharing her love of art. Her current passion is photography on the family farm. Karen's photography is inspired by the beauty of nature.

Galen Cunningham lives in Boulder, Colorado where he is the single father of a bright four-year-old boy. His poetry has appeared in *Literary Yard, The Creativity Magazine,* and *Blue Unicorn* (forthcoming).

Suzanna C. de Baca is a native Iowan, proud Latina, author and artist. A member of the Iowa Writers' Collaborative, her poetry has or will soon be published in: *Etched Onyx Magazine; Wholeness: A Wising Up Anthology; Written Tales; Impermanent Earth; Voices de la Luna; Choeofpleirn Press Glacial Hills Review; Choeofpleirn Press Rushing Through the Dark; Best of Choeofpleirn Press, Our Silent Voices Anthology; Black Fox Literary Magazine; iō Literary Review; Yellow Arrow Press; The Letter Review; Way Words Literary Journal; Telling Magazine;* and *Plate of Pandemics.* She lives in the small rural town of Huxley, Iowa, population 4244.

Margaret Laird Dornin (1916-1968,) was a Pittsburgh painter known for her abstract oils and watercolors. Her work has hung in Pennsylvania museums alongside pieces by Picasso and Klee. Readers can find a score of her paintings still posted online at an art auctioneer's website by googling M. Laird Dornin.

Christopher L. Dornin won 22 New England and New Hampshire press association awards, ending his journalism career as a N.H. Statehouse reporter. He majored in English at Williams College and taught at the high school level for a decade. The poet has published a score of poems in small journals, while earning a N.H. Arts Council fellowship in poetry. He was a runner-up in the 2023 Swan Scythe Chapbook contest. He keeps sending his first full-length book of poems to contests, hoping someone else will publish it for him at age 77.

Chloë Evans-Cross is a Brooklyn-based educator who grew up in South Florida. In the summer of 2023, after focusing on her high school students' writing, she decided to dip back into her own. She has published in *Visit Florida* and has forthcoming pieces in *Hii Magazine, Drunk Monkeys*, and *Cathexis Northwest Press*. She's a fan of the comma splice.

George Freek's poem "Enigmatic Variations" was recently nominated for Best of the Net. His poem "Night Thoughts" was also nominated for a Pushcart Prize. His collection *Melancholia* is published by Red Wolf Editions.

John Grey is an Australian poet, US resident, recently published in *New World Writing, California Quarterly,* and *Lost Pilots*. Latest books, *Between Two Fires, Covert,* and *Memory Outside the Head* are available through Amazon. Work upcoming in *Isotrope Literary Journal, Seventh Quarry, La Presa,* and *Doubly Mad.*

Carol Hamilton has retired from teaching 2nd grade through graduate school in Connecticut, Indiana and Oklahoma, from storytelling and volunteer medical translating. She is a former Poet Laureate of Oklahoma and has published 19 books and chapbooks: children's novels, legends and poetry. She has been nominated ten times for a Pushcart Prize. She has won a Southwest Book Award, Oklahoma Book Award, David Ray Poetry Prize, *Byline Magazine* literary awards in both short story and poetry, Warren Keith Poetry Award, Pegasus Award and a *Chiron Review* Chapbook Award, Editor's Choice Book for *Main Street Rag.*

Susan Harrison is a retired attorney. In 2016, she published a historical novel set in Pakistan, *Beneath a Shooting Star,* under the pseudonym Susan Harrison Rashid. The novel was a 2017 finalist for four awards, including the Connecticut Book Award. She currently lives in Connecticut with her husband.

Robert Harlow resides in upstate New York. A professional stilt walker, he also teaches juggling, fire eating, and other circus arts. His poems appear in *The Midwest Quarterly, Cottonwood, Poetry Northwest, RHINO Poetry,* and in other journals. He is the author of *Places Near and Far* (Louisiana Literature, 2018), or so he has been led to believe.

A retired language arts teacher, **Nancy Haskett's** work has been seen in more than 40 publications, including *Homestead Review, Iodine Press, Miller's Pond, Monterey Poetry Review, Pen Woman magazine, Choeofpleirn Press, Wild Roof Journal,* and many others. She has presented her poetry at the Carnegie Arts Center in Turlock, the Modesto City Council chambers, Second Tuesday Readings at the Barkin' Dog in Modesto, as well as other places. Nancy enjoys reading, traveling, walking/hiking, and spending time with her family. A collection of her poetry, *Shadows and Reflections*, is available to purchase on Amazon.

Greta Holt is the recipient of two Ohio Arts Council Individual Artist Fellowships in fiction. She has published stories in literary magazines and anthologies, including the *Southern Indiana Review*, *Tulip Tree Review*, *A Plate of Pandemic*, and *What Mennonites Are Thinking*. Her website is: https://gretaholtwriter.com. She is working on a collection about Botswana, where her parents worked as educators in the early 1980s.

Marcia L. Hurlow's first full-length collection of poems, *Anomie*, won the Edges Prize. {It also includes a blurb by Paul Zimmer--I'm also a fan!-- from his review of an earlier chapbook in *Georgia Review*.} She also has five award-winning chapbooks. Her individual poems have appeared in *Poetry*, *Poetry Northwest*, *Chicago Review*, *Poetry East*, *Baltimore Review*, *Poetry South*, *The Louisville Review*, *River Styx*, *Zone 3,* and *Kairos*, among others. She is co-editor of *Kansas City Voices*.

E.H. Jacobs is a writer and psychologist in Massachusetts. His work has appeared in *Glacial Hills Review*, *Coneflower Cafe*, *Streetlight Magazine*, *Bryant Literary Review*, *Abandoned Mine*, *Santa Fe Literary Review*, *Permafrost Magazine*, *Hawaii Pacific Review*, *Aji Magazine*, and elsewhere. He was a contributing book review editor of the *American Journal of Psychotherapy* and a Fellow and Clinical Instructor at Harvard Medical School. He has published two books on parenting and several papers in psychology. He was a finalist in the Derick Burleson Poetry Contest and the Phil Heldrich Nonfiction Contest and is a nominee for the Nina Riggs Poetry Award.

Arya F. Jenkins is a Colombian-American poet and writer whose poems have appeared in many journals and zines, most recently *The Ekphrastic Review*, *Hawaii Pacific Review*, *Jerry Jazz Musician*, *OyeDrum Magazine*, and *Reverie Magazine*. Her poetry has been nominated for the Pushcart Prize and has been widely anthologized. She is the author of four poetry chapbooks, a short story collection, *Blue Songs in an Open Key* (Fomite Press), and a novel, *Punk Disco Bohemian* (NineStar Press). Her latest poetry chapbook is *Singing in the Dark* (Alien Buddha Press, 2022).

Craig Kirchner thinks of poetry as hobo art, loves storytelling and the aesthetics of the paper and pen. He has had two poems nominated for the Pushcart, and has a book of poetry, *Roomful of Navels*. After a writing hiatus he was recently published in *Decadent Review*, *New World Writing*, *Wild Violet*, *Ink in Thirds*, *Last Leaves*, *Literary Heist*, *Ariel Chart*, *Lit Shark*, *Cape Magazine*, *Flora Fiction*, *Young Ravens*, *Chiron Review*, *Valiant Scribe*, *Punk Monk* and several dozen other journals.

David Larsen is a writer who lives in El Paso, Texas. His stories and poems have been published in more than thirty-five literary journals and magazines including Aethlon, Floyd County Moonshine, Oakwood, Cholla Needles, The Heartland Review and Change Seven.

Richard Lehan is a short story writer and essayist living in Massachusetts. Most recently, his story "Lipoma" appeared in *Story Sanctum* in December 2023 and was included in their year-end anthology, "Tales from the Vault."

Amy Lerman lives with her husband and cats in the Arizona desert where she is residential English Faculty at Mesa Community College. Her chapbook, *Orbital Debris,* won the 2022 Jonathan Holden Poetry Chapbook Contest. She has been a Pushcart nominee, and her poems have appeared or are forthcoming in *Atticus Review*, *The Madison Review*, *Radar Poetry*, *Slippery Elm*, *Rattle*, and other publications.

Miriam Manglani lives in Cambridge, Massachusetts with her husband and three children. She graduated with a degree in English from Brandeis University and works full-time as a

Technical Training Manager. Her poems have been published in various magazines and journals including *Sparks of Calliope, Red Eft Review, One Art, Glacial Hills Review,* and *Paterson Literary Review.* Her poem, "They've Come," was a finalist for the Beals Prize for Poetry. Her poetry chapbook, *Ordinary Wonders,* was published by Prolific Press.

Patrick Manning teaches composition in the Department of English at the University of Pittsburgh. He also serves as the Outreach Director in the university's Writing Center. Patrick's critical writing has appeared in *Community Literacy Journal, The Canadian Journal of American Studies, Journal of the Midwest MLA* and elsewhere, and his creative writing has appeared in various places, including the edited collection *Western Pennsylvania Reflections: Stories from the Alleghenies to Lake Erie.* Patrick lives in Pittsburgh with his spouse and two children.

Richard Marranca's manuscript, *Speaking of the Dead: Mummies & Mysteries of Egypt,* will be published by Blydyn Square Books. Last two years: he's had stories in *Coneflower Café, The Raven's Perch Magazine,* and DASH; and poetry in *The Paterson Literature Review.* He produces articles for The Collector.com, Ancient Origins, Popular Archaeology, etc. He, Renah & their child Inanna make films; Covid, A Child's View received awards from the Cranford Film Festival & the London Short Film Festival. He's been awarded a Fulbright to teach at LMU Munich, plus seven NEH study grants. Richard enjoys teaching myth, the ancient world, critical thinking, and creative writing.

Robert McMichael is a former humanities academic and high school English teacher, and was actively involved with the Boise State Writing Project. He's published fiction and essays in a variety of places (*Vassar Review, Coneflower Café, American Music, National Geographic Traveler, Gray's Sporting Journal, Boise Journal*). He lives in rural western Idaho.

Kevin McNamara is a former chemist and science teacher living in Binghamton, NY. He used to work in an environmental testing lab that, as in the story, hosted an informal church gathering on Sunday mornings in its lunch room. All other details are entirely of the author's creation.

Brian Mosher was born in Foxboro, MA, and currently resides in nearby Mansfield. He has self-published 3 books: *One Bad Day Deserves Another* (short stories) and *Moon Shine and Lemon Twists* (poetry), both in 2016; and *The Broken Mosaic* (poetry and prose), in 2021. His poetry chapbook, *Dreams and Other Magic* (2023) was published by Alien Buddha Press. His work has appeared in *Verse Wrights, Written Tales, Oddball Magazine, eMerge, Alien Buddha Zine, Esoterica Magazine* and *Half and One Magazine.* He also maintains a poetry blog, Phlubbermatic: (www.phlubbermatic.blogspot.com).

Devon Neal (he/him) is a Kentucky-based poet whose work has appeared in many publications, including *HAD, Livina Press, The Storms,* and *The Bombay Lit Mag,* and has been nominated for *Best of the Net.* He currently lives in Bardstown, Kentuck with his wife and three children.

Claudio Parentela is an illustrator, painter, digital painter, photographer, mail artist, cartoonist, collagist, and freelance journalist. He collaborates with many magazines and comics around the world. See his website for more: https://ilrattobavoso.altervista.org/something-on-me/.

Lynn Pattison's work has appeared in *Smartish Pace, The Notre Dame Review, Slipstream, Tinderbox, The Lake,* and *Moon City Review,* among others, and been anthologized in several venues. She is the author of four poetry collections. *Matryoshka Houses,* debuted in 2020 (Kelsay Press).

Deborah Ann Percy writes and publishes fiction, drama, nonfiction, and translations. Her collection of short fiction, *Cool Front: Stories from Lake Michigan*, was published by March Street Press in 2010. She often collaborates on works with her husband, Arnold Johnston. She retired in 1997 to write full time.

Jordyn-Elizabeth Pimental is an honors college student studying Environmental Science in coastal Massachusetts. When she is not listening to the nearby Atlantic while paddleboarding or crafting stories while writing it is almost a guarantee she is taking pictures of birds. Having an obsession with the natural world, Jordyn is happy to express her love for the planet by taking pictures of it.

Susan Pollet is a published author, emerging poet, visual artist and former public interest lawyer. Her concern for women, children and families has been the paramount driver of her career in all of its forms as well as of her advocacy for women's bar associations.

John RC Potter is an international educator from Canada, living in Istanbul. He has experienced a revolution (Indonesia), air strikes (Israel), earthquakes (Turkey), boredom (UAE), and blinding snow blizzards (Canada), the last being the subject of his story, "Snowbound in the House of God" (*Memoirist*, May 2023). His poems, stories, essays, and reviews have been published in a range of magazines and journals, most recently in *Blank Spaces*, ("In Search of Alice Munro", June 2023), *Literary Yard* ("She Got What She Deserved", June 2023), *Freedom Fiction* ("The Mystery of the Dead-as-a-Doornail Author", July 2023), *The Serulian* ("The Memory Box", September 2023), *The Montreal Review* ("Letter from Istanbul", November 2023) & *Erato Magazine* ("A Day in May 1965"). The author's story, "Ruth's World" (*Fiction on the Web*, March 2023) was nominated for the prestigious Pushcart Prize. His first full-length publication will be the gay-themed children's picture book, *The First Adventures of Walli and Magoo*, to be published in 2024.

Jane Richards' poetry has appeared in numerous journals, including *Glacial Hills Review, After Hours, Gyroscope Review,* and *Willow Review.* Her work has been included in *The Best of Choeofpleirn Press* and she has been nominated for a Pushcart prize. Her chapbook, *The Feather Variations*, will be published in spring, 2024. A retired piano teacher, she now pursues her life-long passions for writing, nature and travel. She holds masters degrees in social work and creative writing.

Sarah Selim is an Egyptian-American artist and writer, with over 15 published posts on her blog 'Scout E.S. in the Shadows'. She is currently a student and resides in Northern Virginia with her family of eight. The biggest inspiration behind her work is the combination of religion, culture, and experience. When she isn't thinking about her overdue assignments, you will most likely find her painting or playing the saxophone. Sarah has been published in CelebratingArt and TeenInk and was featured in Britepaths' Annual Artful Living Exhibit. The young creator's goal is to survive society with as few enemies as possible.

Corinna Underwood is a British author currently residing in Rome, Georgia. As well as numerous poems and short stories, she have published two non-fiction books, Murder and Mystery in Atlanta and Haunted History of Atlanta and North Georgia, and three fiction mysteries with a paranormal twist, A Walk On The Darkside, Beyond The Darkside, and Return To The Darkside.

Mark Walsh is an English professor at Massasoit Community College in Brockton, Massachusetts, where he teaches literature and philosophy. He is a submissions reader for *The Lily Poetry Review*, and his book reviews have appeared in the *Lily Poetry Review* and *Solstice*.

His poetry publications include *Beatnik Cowboy, Lily Poetry Review, Wilderness House Literary Review,* and *Abandoned Mine.*

Jennifer Weigel is a multi-disciplinary mixed media conceptual artist. Weigel utilizes a wide range of media to convey her ideas, including assemblage, drawing, fibers, installation, jewelry, painting, performance, photography, sculpture, video and writing. Much of her work touches on themes of beauty, identity (especially gender identity), memory & forgetting, and institutional critique. Weigel's art has been exhibited nationally in all 50 states and has won numerous awards. Find more of her work at the following websites:
> Fine Art: https://www.jenniferweigelart.com/;
> Conceptual Projects: https://www.jenniferweigelprojects.com/;
> Public Art: https://jenniferweigelpublicart.blogspot.com/;
> Writing: https://jenniferweigelwords.wordpress.com/.

Buff Whitman-Bradley's book *At the Driveway Guitar Sale: Poems on Aging, Memory, Mortality,* was published in 2021 by Main Street Rag Publishers. His books *The Heron Could Be Lost* (Finishing Line Press) and *And What Will We Sing?* (Kelsay Books) were published in 2022. His podcast of poems on aging can be heard at thirdactpoems.podbean.com. He lives in northern California with his wife, Cynthia.

Cheri Williams has weathered many trials in her life and has traveled many roads, but she has a green thumb that is the envy of everyone who knows her. Luckily for us, she also takes photos of many of the plants she grows. She finally found the love of her life in a furry little friend she calls Mia.

Hannah Woodvine is a writer, English Teacher and poet living in Brighton, England. As a child, she won national competitions for her short stories, which appeared in anthologies by Chapter One Promotions and The Reader's Digest. Since leaving behind sleepy hippos for poetry and speculative fiction, she has had two short stories published by *The Chamber Magazine*, with a third upcoming with *Crow and Cross Keys*. Her poetry has been published by *Flight of the Dragonfly*, earned her second place at Ledbury Poetry Festival's 2023 Slam, and a place in the final of Hammer and Tongue Brighton's 2023 Slam.

Ads

Listening for Low Tide

Available at Amazon and
Choeofpleirn Press

Too much happens at ground level:
the kids selling candy or delivering
newspapers shortcut through the yard,
the neighbors' dogs blare their alarms
in unison, and teens, shielded by the heartbeat
of their music, speed down the street.

Two stories above the ground.
I welcome the afternoon sunlight
as it stretches across the rug,
my cat moving with it. From the opposite
window, the shadows cast by trees
overspread the ground, the sunlight only
hitting the treetops. Sound waves lap
against the building, the tide at its lowest
each night when the owl in the park
starts to hoot its presence.

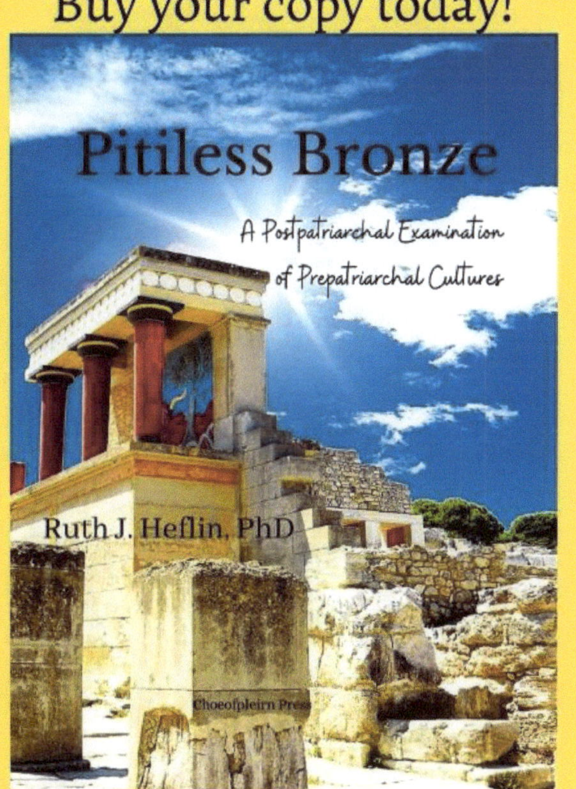

When did humanity learn that men have a
biological role in pregnancy?

What did our ancient ancestors believe about
Female Magic
prior to learning of procreation?

How did men go about appropriating women's
superior spiritual powers
for themselves?

Dr. Heflin answers these questions
and more!

Available whereever books are sold.

Thank You
for reading Coneflower Cafe
Choeofpleirn Press
www.choeofpleirnpress.com

FUN
FACT
CHOEOFPLEIRN
IS A COMBINATION OF OUR
SURNAMES BY ALTERNATING
LETTERS

www.choeofpleirnpress.com

THE MARY
CASSATT AWARD
FOR ART
Choeofpleirn Press

www.ingramcontent.com/pod-product-compliance
Lightning Source LLC
Chambersburg PA
CBHW041417300726
48978CB00003B/126